Lena's L.

GET ALL THIS FREE
WITH JUST ONE PROOF OF PURCHASE:

$50 VALUE

◆ **Hotel Discounts** up to 60% at home and abroad ◆ **Travel Service -** Guaranteed lowest published airfares plus 5% cash back on tickets ◆ **$25 Travel Voucher** ◆ **Sensuous Petite Parfumerie** collection ◆ **Insider Tips Letter** with sneak previews of upcoming books

You'll get a FREE personal card, too. It's your passport to all these ben-fi even more great

There's no club to join. No p

Enrollment Form

☐ *Yes!* I WANT TO BE A *Privileged Woman.*
Enclosed is one *PAGES & PRIVILEGES™* Proof of
Purchase from any Harlequin or Silhouette book currently for
sale in stores (Proofs of Purchase are found on the back pages
of books) and the store cash register receipt. Please enroll me
in *PAGES & PRIVILEGES™*. Send my Welcome Kit and FREE
Gifts -- and activate my FREE benefits -- immediately.

More great gifts and benefits to come.

"I love watching you nurse him," Chase said

He leaned over and outlined the curve of the baby's cheek with one finger. "Maybe you were flirting with me last night. Or maybe you were just acting natural. Whichever it was, I'd never want you to be embarrassed about doing this in front of me."

"For some reason, I haven't been," Amanda murmured.

"Good." He traced a path along Bartholomew's chin and continued the caress over the fullness of Amanda's breast. She gasped and looked up at him.

His gaze was fathomless as he continued to trace soft patterns over her breast. "I've never wanted a woman the way I want you," he said softly. "I haven't wanted to admit that, but it's true. You're driving me crazy."

She had trouble breathing. "Chase, we can't—"

"I know." He glanced down at Bartholomew. "But I couldn't resist touching you, just this once." He moved away from her with a sigh. "And once is all I can manage without forgetting myself."

Dear Reader,

Walk into any truck stop and chances are you'll hear country music on the radio and see truckers wearing Western shirts and boots. No modern occupation seems to resemble the life of an old-time cowboy as much as trucking, so it wasn't much of a stretch for me to imagine Chase Lavette giving up his Peterbilt for a cow pony. His life as a drifter fit perfectly into the rhythm of the West.

Chase embodies a double fantasy. I've always been intrigued by eighteen-wheelers and the men who drive them—anybody remember the old television show "B.J. and the Bear," or more recently, the Sylvester Stallone movie *Over the Top*? If you start with a trucker who is drop-dead gorgeous and then transform him into an honest-to-goodness cowboy who rides and ropes, what more could you ask for? Especially when all that raging masculinity is contrasted with Chase's tenderness when he holds his baby son. So prepare yourself for a wild ride, or as Chase would say, "Get in, sit down, shut up and hang on."

Happy trails,

Vicki Lewis Thompson

Vicki Lewis Thompson
THE DRIFTER

Harlequin Books

TORONTO • NEW YORK • LONDON
AMSTERDAM • PARIS • SYDNEY • HAMBURG
STOCKHOLM • ATHENS • TOKYO • MILAN
MADRID • WARSAW • BUDAPEST • AUCKLAND

For my editor, Susan Sopcek,
without whom there would have been no series.

ISBN 0-373-25659-0

THE DRIFTER

Copyright © 1995 by Vicki Lewis Thompson.

This edition published by arrangement with Harlequin Books S.A.

® and TM are trademarks of the publisher. Trademarks indicated with
® are registered in the United States Patent and Trademark Office, the
Canadian Trade Marks Office and in other countries.

Printed in U.S.A.

Prologue

JUST BEFORE the elevator reversed direction and plummeted to the basement, Chase Lavette was thinking about Amanda Drake. Had she become pregnant that night they'd spent in his truck? Surely she would have contacted him by now. Yet he couldn't shake off the suspicion that she might not, and he'd finally decided to see for himself. There was no way she'd be able to hide the fact at eight months. He didn't welcome the idea of being a dad, but he'd really hate to be one and not know it.

Without warning, a relay failed between the second and third floors, catapulting the elevator toward the bottom at a thousand feet per minute. Chase had approximately three seconds to wish Amanda's office had been on ground level. He looked around and met the startled gaze of the two men who shared the elevator with him: a business type and a New York City cop. He swore once, loudly, just before the elevator slammed into its concrete base. It felt as though somebody had swung a sledgehammer against the balls of his feet as he went down, pain knifing through his spine.

1

HE WAS ALIVE. Twenty years ago, a social worker had told Chase he was a survivor, and apparently the lady had called it right. He started to move and clenched his teeth in pain. He was alive, but something major was wrong with his back.

The air was hot and close. It even smelled hot, like sizzled circuits. He strained to hear any sound of movement from the other two men in the darkness of the crumpled elevator car. Nothing. His stomach felt as if he'd stripped a gear. He'd seen fatalities on the highway, plenty of them, but that hadn't made the prospect of death easier to handle. Still, he was conscious and they didn't seem to be. It was up to him to help.

The groan of stressed metal discouraged him from trying to get up. Then somebody coughed. Thank God. They weren't both dead. "Who's that?" he asked, his throat rusty from fear.

"Name's McGuinnes." A pause. "T. R. McGuinnes. You?"

"Chase Lavette. Are you the cop?"

"No."

Chase grimaced. The cop would probably be of more use than some Wall Street paper pusher. "Do you think he's dead?"

"I hope to God he's not. Are you hurt?"

"Yeah. Something's wrong with my back. It hurts like hell. How about you?"

"I hit my head. Listen, you'd better not move. I'll check the cop."

Chase had no intention of moving if somebody else was volunteering to be the hero. Damn, it would have to be his back. A trucker's nightmare. Of course, the cop might be dead, a thought that put his back problems into perspective real quick. He listened as McGuinnes crawled across the buckled floor of the elevator. As Chase's vision adjusted a little to the darkness, he noticed that the ceiling had partially collapsed and a light fixture dangled near the floor. His heart pounded as if he'd been running and his sweaty T-shirt stuck to his chest. "It's getting damned hot in here," he said.

"Yeah."

"They should be coming to get us out pretty soon." Chase said it more to reassure himself than anything.

"Let's hope so."

Chase held his breath as McGuinnes moved toward the cop.

"If you try mouth-to-mouth resuscitation, you're a dead man," mumbled a voice.

Chase relaxed against the wall, feeling giddy with relief. Thank God there wouldn't be any corpses in this elevator.

"Never learned it, anyway," McGuinnes said, handing the cop a handkerchief out of his pocket. "Here. You're bleeding somewhere."

The cop sounded weary. "No joke. How's the other guy?"

"I'll survive," Chase said.

"Says his back hurts," McGuinnes added. "I told him not to move."

"Good," the cop said. "Moving a back-injury case and severing his spinal cord would top this episode off nicely." The cop pushed himself to a sitting position. "That briefcase cut the hell out of my chin. What's that thing made of, steel?"

"Brass trim," McGuinnes said.

Chase rolled his eyes.

There was a snort from the cop. "You got a cellular phone in it, at least?"

"Yeah."

"Then you'd better use it," the cop said. "This has been great fun, but I'm due back at the station in an hour."

"I suppose almost getting killed is a big yawner for you, isn't it?" McGuinnes asked.

"Killed in an elevator accident?" the cop said. "You've been seeing too many Keanu Reeves movies. New York elevators are safer than your grandmother's rocking chair."

"Tell that to my back," Chase said. "I can't drive with a busted back, and if I can't drive, I can't pay off my rig." He thought of the black Peterbilt 379—all-aluminum hood, stainless-steel grille, Cummins 500E engine. It held a shine like patent leather and handled like the thoroughbred it was. Silver pinstriping on the cab door announced his CB handle—*The Drifter*. Eight months he'd had it. The rig had been a bare three days old when he'd rescued Amanda Drake from a snowdrift in Upstate New York, and Amanda had helped him christen it, in a way.

"If you can't drive, you'll get an insurance settlement," McGuinnes told him.

Chase pulled his thoughts away from that long, snowbound night with Amanda and considered the situation. McGuinnes was probably right. He grimaced. He couldn't imagine life without a gray ribbon of road unwinding in front of him. "And sit around doing nothing? No thanks."

While McGuinnes contacted 911, Chase thought about Amanda, working in some office above him at this very moment. It looked as if he wouldn't be able to see her, after all. He'd ignored her wishes by coming here, but he just wanted to be absolutely sure she wasn't eight months' pregnant with his baby. Or maybe that was the excuse he gave himself because he craved another look at that bonfire of red hair that tumbled past her shoulders. He could still feel it bunched in his fist, still see the light in her blue eyes just before he'd kissed her.

"They're sending a team to get us out," McGuinnes said, snapping the phone closed.

Chase had just opened his mouth to say that was good, when the elevator rumbled and lurched to the right. "Damn!" he yelled. "Aren't we all the way down yet?"

"We're all the way down," the cop said. "The blasted thing's still settling, that's all. Move all your fingers and toes, see if you still have your motor coordination."

Chase felt dizzy at the thought of paralysis. He almost didn't want to put the idea to the test, but he had to know. He wiggled his right hand, his left, and both feet. Then he closed his eyes in gratitude. "I can move everything," he said.

"Good," the cop said. "What's your name?"

"Lavette. Chase Lavette."

"T. R. McGuinnes," the guy in the suit said.

"Joe Gilardini," the cop added, completing the introductions. "I wish I could say it was nice to meet you guys, but under the circumstances I wish I'd been denied the pleasure."

"Same here," Chase said.

McGuinnes remained silent. "Either one of you ever been out West?" he asked finally.

Chase's eyes snapped open. What an off-the-wall question. "Why do you want to know?"

"I don't, really. I just think talking is better than sitting around waiting for the elevator to shift again."

Chase understood the logic. "Guess you're right. No, I've never been out West. Eastern Seaboard's my route." He decided it was up to him to add something to the conversation. "Always wanted to go out there, though."

The cop sighed. "God, so have I. The wide-open spaces. Peace and quiet."

"No elevators," Chase added, trying to lighten things up.

"Yeah," the cop said. "If I didn't have my kid living in New York, I'd turn in my badge, collect my pension and go."

All three were silent for a while, and Chase decided that was the end of the chitchat.

"I just heard about this guest ranch in Arizona that's up for sale," McGuinnes said a few minutes later. "One of those working guest ranches with a small herd of cattle. I'm going out there next week to look it over."

That got Chase's attention. He'd always wished he knew somebody who owned a ranch. "No kidding? Think you might buy it?"

"If it checks out."

"Running a guest ranch," the cop mused out loud. "You know, that wouldn't be half-bad."

"And after I've had some fun with it, I'll sell it for a nice profit. The city's growing in that direction, and in a couple of years developers will be crying to get their hands on that land, all one hundred and sixty acres of it. I can't lose."

"A hundred and sixty acres," Chase said, letting his mind play with it. He loved open spaces.

"I'm looking for partners."

A ranch, Chase thought. Riding the range, roping cattle, camping under the stars. Chase hadn't called himself *The Drifter* by accident. He was a city boy and had never imagined he could be anything else, but the life of a trucker came about as close to riding the range as anything he could imagine.

The cop laughed. "Now I've heard everything. Only in New York would a guy use an accident as a chance to set up a deal."

The elevator settled with another metallic groan.

"Would you rather sit here and think about the elevator collapsing on us?" McGuinnes asked.

"I'd rather think about your ranch," Chase said. "I'd go in on it in a minute if I had the cash."

"You might get that settlement," McGuinnes said.

"You know, I might." He'd hate to sell his rig, but if he had to, then buying into a ranch might take the sting out of it. "Listen, McGuinnes, after we get out of here, let's keep in touch. You never know."

"I guarantee you wouldn't go wrong with this investment. The Sun Belt's booming."

"I think you're both nutcases," the cop said.

"So you're not interested?" McGuinnes asked.

"I didn't say that. Hell, what else is there to be interested in down in this hole? If the ranch looks good, just call the Forty-third Precinct and leave a message for me."

McGuinnes stirred. "Let me get some business cards out of my briefcase."

"I'd just as soon not think about your briefcase, McGuinnes," Gilardini said.

Chase smiled. Gilardini was okay.

"Let's talk some more about the ranch," Gilardini continued. "What's the name of it, anyway? I always liked those old ranch names—the Bar X, the Rocking J. Remember 'Bonanza'?"

"I saw that on reruns," Chase said. "The guy I liked was Clint Eastwood. I snuck in to see *High Plains Drifter* at least six times when I was a kid. Back then, I would have given anything to be a cowboy."

"Yeah, me, too," Gilardini admitted. "So what's the place called?"

McGuinnes didn't answer right away. "Well, this spread is named something a little different," he said at last.

"Yeah?" Gilardini said. "What could be so different?"

"The True Love Ranch."

COMING UP WITH the ad copy for the Russian Tea Room wasn't going well. Amanda had felt queasy since five that morning, and detailing the wonders of blini and borscht didn't help. She'd also had abdominal twinges, but it was too early for labor pains—a good four weeks too early. Dismissing the twinges, she focused on her computer screen.

By noon the pain had become more intense, and she laid a hand on her swollen belly. "Stop it, Bartholomew," she lectured. "Go back to sleep so I can finish this copy." She couldn't in good conscience feel sorry for herself. She'd chosen to accept this complication in her life, and most of the time she felt like a kid waiting for Christmas. An ultrasound had provided knowledge of the baby's sex, and she had everything ready, from his name to his non-gender-specific nursery. No son of hers would grow up to be a male chauvinist.

Her desk phone buzzed just as another pain hit. She grimaced and reached for the receiver.

"A call for you from a Mr. Chase Lavette," said Bonnie, the receptionist. "He won't say what it's in reference to. Do you want to take it?"

Fear closed her throat. So he'd tracked her down, after all. She'd been a fool to tell him where she worked, but that had been before things had become . . . more personal. Thank God he'd called instead of coming to see her. And she'd better take the call, or he might show up on her doorstep.

"I think he has something to do with the Big Brothers campaign we're putting together," Amanda said, trying to sound casual so as not to create more interest. "I'll take it." She didn't want anyone in the office to remember the name of Chase Lavette.

"I'll put him through, then."

Bracing herself, Amanda listened to the phone line click open.

"Amanda?"

His voice took her by storm. At the sound of it, everything came back—the terror as her Mercedes slid into a snowbank, the relief at being rescued by somebody in a huge black truck and the excitement of being snowbound in the cab all night with a man like Chase, the type of guy she'd never had reason to know before and never expected to see again.

"Hello, Chase," she said. Another pain ran through her abdomen and she winced. "What a surprise."

"Listen, I was on my way up to your office this morning and the craziest thing happened."

Her glance swung to the door, half expecting him to walk in at any moment. She had to keep him away.

"The elevator crashed," he continued. "I'm in the hospital and something's wrong with my back."

She sagged against her chair in relief, then immediately bolted upright as she realized that her reaction wasn't appropriate. "That's terrible," she said. "Are you in a lot of pain?" Another spasm took her breath away.

"It's not so bad. I thought I'd broken something, but it could just be muscle damage. They've given me stuff for the pain. You know, Amanda, I haven't been able to get that night we spent together out of my mind."

Damn! Just what she'd been afraid of. "Really? I'd practically forgotten until you called just now."

He was silent.

She'd hurt him, but she couldn't help it. She didn't dare tell him that she'd never had such great sex in her life and that she'd forever compare other men to him when it came to lovemaking. She couldn't give him that information, because he might decide to renew the acquaintance, and she couldn't afford to see him again. A sense of obligation might make him insist on things—marriage, perhaps, or a role in raising Bartholomew. "Well, if you'll excuse me, I need to get back to work." She gritted her teeth to keep from moaning as another pain twisted within her. "Nice of you to call."

"Dammit, Amanda, I have to know." His gentle tone had been replaced with the macho snap she would expect from a trucker. "A condom's never broken on me before. Did you get pregnant that night?"

"I said I'd let you know if I did." She gripped the edge of her desk as sweat beaded on her forehead.

"Yes, you did, but I—you didn't have an abortion, did you?"

"No." She'd debated the issue until it was too late.

"Look, I just want to take care of my responsibilities."

"Well, you have none."

"Apparently not." There was a note of regret in his voice. "Sorry to have bothered you, Amanda."

"Goodbye, Chase." She hung up, disconnecting herself from the father of her child just as her water broke.

THREE WEEKS LATER, Chase stood in the lobby of Amanda's office building staring at the elevator. Except for the hospital elevators, where he'd been strapped to a gurney and given no choice but to ride, he hadn't been inside one since the accident. He didn't much like the idea now, but the Artemis Advertising Agency was on the twentieth floor.

His back was behaving itself today. When the spasms hit, he was damn near immobilized, but this morning he'd felt so good he decided to finish his original mission—to find out if Amanda was pregnant. Yet, after fifteen minutes of watching people surge in and out of the elevator, he was no more ready to ride than when he'd walked into the lobby. He glanced around, found the sign for the stairs and was halfway across the lobby when he paused. Then, with a muttered oath of resolution, he strode back to the elevator just before the doors closed, shoved them open and stepped inside.

The trip up made his stomach pitch. He glared suspiciously at the three women and four men in the elevator with him and wondered if any of them would be prepared with a cellular phone in case of an emergency. His jaw clenched, he watched the flashing numbers above the door. When the twentieth floor appeared, he wanted to shoulder his way past the others who were getting off, but he held back, forcing himself to face the fear. Once free of the elevator, he flexed his shoulders with a sigh and a little smile of triumph. He'd ridden the damn thing.

He stuck his head in the first office that bore the Artemis name on the door and flashed the famous Lavette grin complete with dimple. "I'm looking for Amanda Drake."

The receptionist, a woman in her forties, reacted as most women did when he smiled at them. Pink rose to her cheeks, and the pupils of her eyes widened. Chase had had that effect on women ever since he'd reached puberty, and it was a nice perk in a life that hadn't presented all that many.

"Do you know where I might find her?" he prompted, knowing that sometimes women took a moment to pull themselves together before they answered. According to the nameplate on her desk, this one was named Bonnie Chalmers.

She blinked. "Miss Drake's on extended leave," she said as if reciting her times tables.

Chase thought that over. There was one obvious reason for her to be on extended leave, but his trucking buddies had told him that women in this day and age didn't slip off quietly and have babies. They demanded child support, his buddies had said, and plenty of it.

"She's not sick or anything, is she, Bonnie?" Chase asked.

At the use of her name, Bonnie flushed pinker. "No, she's fine. She'll just be out of the office for a while."

It was all very mysterious, Chase thought, but he didn't know how things worked in the city. He had no doubt Amanda had a high-powered career, both from what she'd told him on that snowy night, and from the evidence of her material success. He'd noted the late-model Mercedes first. Then he'd caught a whiff of unfamiliar cologne, which he'd later identified by checking out a display in Lord and Taylor.

Then there was the matter of her clothes. He'd had the pleasure of discovering the softness of her cashmere coat as he'd taken it off. He hadn't been paying attention to labels when he'd removed her wool suit and silk blouse, but later, when the clothes were lying around the cab, he'd noticed names like Calvin Klein and Chanel. And her underwear... he could still get aroused thinking about those fragile scraps of lace that had to have been imported from Paris. Maybe she was in Europe right this minute, picking up more of that fancy underwear.

He walked over to the desk. "I guess I'll just leave her a message, then."

"That would be fine. Do you have a card?"

Chase laughed. "No, Bonnie. I don't even have a piece of paper. Is there something I could write on?"

"Certainly." She whipped the top page from a notepad beside her telephone and held it out to him, along with a pen. "I'm sure she'll be sorry she missed you."

Chase wished he could be as sure about that as Bonnie. Amanda had been very cool three weeks ago when he'd called. But three weeks ago he'd simply been a trucker, and an injured one, at that. Today, his back was slowly mending, and soon he might be part owner in a ranch. In a few years, according to McGuinnes, he could be rich. That prospect had given him the courage to come here to issue an invitation to Amanda to come out to Arizona as his guest.

He hoped she would, even though she'd told him straight-out that she didn't think they had anything in common besides sex. And she was probably right. It was a damn strong suit, though. He'd made love to a lot of women, and he'd had a pleasant time with most of them. Yet that night with Amanda had shaken him to a depth he'd never reached with anyone. Her eyes, her soft body and her flame-colored hair had haunted him during eight months of long nights on the road. Knowing that Amanda would probably reject him if he asked her out, he'd tried to forget her with a lusty waitress in Atlanta and a sophisticated bartender in Hartford. And still he burned.

AS THE 747 cruised on in to Tucson International Airport, Amanda jiggled Bartholomew in her arms in an attempt to stop his wailing. This was such a bad idea, she thought, looking down at the desert, which at this altitude looked like the browned top of a crumb cake just out of the oven. The pilot had already announced the temperature in Tucson—one hundred and five degrees. She hated to think of how the heat would affect her, let alone a two-month-old baby.

But she had a problem, one she hadn't figured out a way to solve except by coming here. Her family had been shocked and embarrassed by the news of her pregnancy, but her concocted story of going to a sperm bank to get pregnant on purpose had mollified them. That had a classier ring to it than the word *accident*, not to mention the longer version of the truth—a one-night stand with a trucker. Her story had remained viable until the day little Clare, daughter of her best friend, Janice, was diagnosed with diabetes.

"Thank God we knew what to look for," Janice had said when she broke the news. "It runs in the family, so we got on it right away."

In that moment, Amanda's carefully constructed house of cards had tumbled down. This little dark-haired imp who in the past two months had become the center of her world could have a predisposition for any number of life-threatening diseases. She couldn't position herself as his protector unless she knew what to fight. Only one person had the answers—the person waiting in the terminal to take her out to the True Love Guest Ranch.

His move to Arizona had been a convenient one for her. Living so far away, he was less of a threat to her independence, and she could come out here, question him and return to New York without anyone back home being the wiser. She hadn't told Chase about the baby when she'd written her letter telling him of her impending arrival. She didn't think it was the sort of thing one revealed in a letter.

But now, as the plane's wheels bumped against the runway, she wished she had. The prospect of meeting Chase again for the first time since that snowy night was nerve-racking enough. To meet him while carrying his child in her arms might be more than either of them could handle.

The plane taxied to the gate and Bartholomew stopped crying for the first time in two hours. Amanda remained in her seat fussing with his blanket and checking his diaper while passengers filed past her. At last she and the baby were alone with the flight attendants and she had no choice but to gather him in her arms, hoist the diaper bag over her shoulder and start that long walk down the jetway.

She paused at the door of the plane and looked into Bartholomew's blue eyes that already held a hint of green, like Chase's. "Well, kid," she said, taking a deep breath. "Time to meet your daddy."

2

CHASE SHIFTED his weight from one booted foot to the other as he watched passengers funnel out of the jetway. Amanda would appear any minute now. He adjusted his hat and flexed his shoulders, feeling like a teenager on a first date, with the same sweaty-palmed excitement, the same nervous hopes for the night ahead. Well, perhaps greater hopes than a teenager on a first date might have, he thought with a smile. After all, he and Amanda had become lovers ten months ago.

Her handwritten note had been short. *If it's convenient, I'd like to take you up on your offer.* Except for listing her flight number and arrival time, that had been it. He couldn't consider it a proposition, exactly, but why else would she come to the ranch? She could afford to vacation anywhere in the world. Copying her style, he'd sent a short note back—*I'll meet your plane.* Maybe he and Amanda didn't need words between them. Their bodies had done most of the talking the night they'd met.

He was glad she hadn't come out six weeks earlier, when he'd first arrived at the ranch. Thanks to laps in the pool and massages by the head wrangler, Leigh Singleton, his back was in much better shape. He would have hated it to spasm at some awkward moment, like in the middle of making love. He'd asked Freddy Singleton, Leigh's sister and the ranch foreman, to reserve the little honeymoon cottage for Amanda. Marriage was the last thing on his mind, but the cottage stood in a mesquite grove several hundred yards from the main house, which gave it lots of privacy. Not as much as the curtained bunk of an 18-wheeler on a snowy night, but more than the guest rooms in the main ranch house.

The steady flow of people from the plane slowed to a trickle. With a sick feeling of disappointment Chase wondered if Amanda had changed her mind. Maybe she'd read the weather reports for Tucson and decided her fair skin wasn't suited for the desert summer. He'd worried about that and had planned to make sure she wore hats and long sleeves when she was outside. In the six weeks he'd been on the ranch, his skin had bronzed to a rich brown, but Amanda's skin was so much more delicate.... He licked dry lips and stood on tiptoe to peer deep into the empty tunnel leading to the plane. Maybe he should ask someone if she'd been on the flight.

Then he saw a flash of red hair as a woman came out of the gloom toward him. His heart hammered in his chest. She looked exactly as he'd remembered, only perhaps more beautiful. Her face had the most wonderful glow to it, and her hair was the color of an Arizona sunset. He'd have to remember to tell her that.

He couldn't see the rest of her very well. She had a large piece of luggage slung over one shoulder and was carrying something, holding it close to her chest. He stared at the bundle. It looked a lot like . . .

The breath rushed out of him and he grabbed the back of a chair for support. Slack-jawed, he stared as the bundle in her arms squirmed. Oh, God. Oh, God!

She came forward slowly, her blue gaze fastened on him.

He braced himself as if standing against a stiff wind. *She'd had a baby! His baby!* An explosion of wonder left him weak and dizzy.

As she drew near, fragments of questions formed and disappeared in his mind like campfire smoke. At last he focused on the fire itself, the burning anger of betrayal.

"Hello, Chase." She sounded out of breath.

Fury made him tremble as he glared down at her. "Liar," he said in a voice gone dead with shock. The baby began to cry.

NOT A GOOD BEGINNING, Amanda thought as she hurried to keep up with Chase's long strides on the way to baggage claim. His expression reminded her of the hurricanes that sometimes buffeted her parents' summer cottage on Long Island. He looked different—taller, more muscular and definitely more tanned than she remembered. The cowboy outfit suited him, but she'd bet his prizewinning smile wouldn't appear today, or the dimple in his cheek that had fascinated her so.

"If you'll let me try to explain," she said, raising her voice above Bartholomew's wailing.

"Not here," he snapped, glancing at the luggage circling the carousel. "What do your suitcases look like?"

"Burgundy leather, Louis Vuitton," she said. "And there's an infant seat, too."

His laugh was harsh. "I suppose that's made by Calvin Klein. All I really had to do was look for the most expensive stuff on the belt."

Amanda turned away to hide the sudden tears that spilled down her face. Here was the true reason behind her plan to keep Bartholomew a secret from Chase. She'd always sensed they wouldn't be able to bridge the social gaps between them. He obviously didn't respect the way she lived and probably the reverse would be true, although she tried not to be a snob. She held her wet cheek against Bartholomew's, and gradually he stopped crying and began to nuzzle against her skin, seeking food.

"Let's go," Chase said from behind her.

She glanced over her shoulder to where he stood hoisting her two large suitcases as if they were filled with air, the infant seat tucked under one arm. She walked toward the entrance, where the sunshine met her like a bank of floodlights.

"Cover the baby," Chase ordered.

"I was planning to." Shielding Bartholomew's face with the blanket, she gasped as they stepped into the ovenlike heat. Landscaping outside the terminal consisted of a few lacy-leaved trees and a desert garden, dominated by a giant cactus that looked like a missile with arms. Amanda had seen pictures of a cactus like that, and she tried to remember its name.

Chase looked over his shoulder before he started across the street. "Don't you have a hat or something?" he asked, his tone brittle.

"No." She lowered her head against the glare. "And my sunglasses are in the diaper bag."

With a deep sigh he set down the suitcases and infant seat before leaning over and opening the bag hanging from her shoulder. The brim of his hat brushed her arm and the air around them filled with the scent of baby powder as he searched through the bag until he located her glasses. He found them, spread the earpieces and slid the glasses over the bridge of her nose. As he leaned close, her gaze dropped to the open neck of his shirt where a small medallion on a pewter chain nestled against a dark swirl of chest hair. She remembered that medallion, remembered thinking it looked vaguely familiar, though she couldn't have said why.

"There." Chase backed away from what under different circumstances might have been a tender moment. A woman passing by looked at them and smiled.

Amanda bit her lip to stifle a little sob of despair. She'd been sniffling a lot lately, and she needed to stop. Her friends with children said crying jags were typical with new mothers, but Amanda didn't want to be typical. Tears were inconvenient and demonstrated far too much vulnerability for her taste. She was a single mother and wanted to keep that status. She had to be tough.

Chase directed them past the cactus garden to a battered van with steer horns where a hood ornament should be. He opened the passenger door where True Love Guest Ranch was stenciled above a heart with an arrow through it. If she'd been in the mood for laughing, Amanda would have gotten a kick out of that. What a joke.

She put one foot on the running board and immediately realized she'd never be able to climb into the van while holding Bartholomew. Then, before she could figure out another way to get in, Chase placed his hands at her waist and lifted her, baby and all, into the seat. And she remembered his touch—a combination of gentleness and strength that had, many months ago, made her beg for his caress.

The interior of the van was stifling, and she loosened the blanket around Bartholomew, who was beginning to squirm and wrinkle his face in preparation for a good long howl of protest. There were two heavy thuds as Chase heaved the luggage into the back of the van and closed the doors.

"I'll strap the infant seat right behind you," he said, coming back to the passenger door and opening the side of the van. "We have child-restraint laws in Arizona. The baby needs to be buckled up."

She turned and watched him secure the infant seat. "I don't need a law to tell me that. How long before we get to the ranch?"

"More than an hour, depending on traffic."

"He's very hungry," she said. "I really should feed him before we start."

Chase's hands stilled. "It's a boy?"

"Yes."

He lowered his head for a moment, without speaking.

"His name's Bartholomew," she ventured.

Slowly, he lifted his head and gazed at her. "Bartholomew what?"

She swallowed. "Drake."

He nodded and turned away to finish securing the infant seat. By the time he climbed behind the wheel of the van, Bartholomew was crying. "I'll get us out of here and find some shade," he muttered, gunning the engine and switching on the air conditioner full blast.

In a few minutes he'd wheeled into the parking lot of a hotel near the airport. Amanda was surprised to see grass and large trees instead of cactus surrounding the hotel. Chase pulled into a shaded parking space near a bubbling fountain and rolled down his window. She shifted a wailing Bartholomew to her left arm and tried to roll down her window, too, but it was stuck.

"Here. I'll do it," Chase said, sounding disgusted as he leaned across her lap and forced the handle until the window lowered. A breeze, cooled by the fountain, wafted in. He straightened, but not before Amanda caught a whiff of his after-shave, a scent she associated exclusively with Chase. The men she usually dated wore designer fragrances. The minty aroma of Chase's inex-

pensive after-shave was now indelibly paired in her mind
with mind-blowing pleasure and powerful climaxes. Just
the faintest trace of that scent could arouse her. It was a
fact she never intended him to know.

"Thank you," she said, reaching for the buttons of her
blouse.

He glanced away as she unfastened her nursing bra and
gave her nipple to Bartholomew, whose cries transformed immediately into soft sucking sounds. Amanda
began to relax a little as the baby nursed. The gentle
breeze and the splash of the nearby fountain suggested
coolness, even if drops of perspiration gathered between her milk-heavy breasts.

She looked at Chase, who stared fixedly out the window, his elbow propped against the opening, his chin in
his hand. "I'm sorry to spring this on you so abruptly,"
she said. "But a phone call or letter didn't seem like the
way to tell you."

"You've known how to reach me ever since that night,"
he said, not looking at her. "We could have met for coffee months ago, if you'd wanted to tell me face-to-face."

"The truth is, I didn't plan to tell you at all."

His jaw tightened. "That sucks, Amanda."

"But I didn't know you!"

Her loud retort startled Bartholomew, who lost his
grasp on her nipple and began to cry. She guided him
back, murmuring assurances. When she looked up,
Chase was watching her, a yearning in his green eyes that
made her catch her breath.

"Didn't you?" he said.

Yes, she'd known him. That night in the truck, she'd
sensed a will of iron, one that would probably have
clashed with hers when it came to this baby. "When I first
found out, I planned to have an abortion," she said.

His whole body went rigid. "Without telling me?" he asked too quietly.

"I was afraid you'd try to talk me out of it."

"So what?" Beneath the mildly voiced question lay a band of steely anger. "I had a right to know, to take part in the decision. I asked for that right, remember? We talked about it, and you promised to tell me if you were pregnant."

She sighed and stroked Bartholomew's downy hair. "Well, as you can see, I couldn't go through with it, anyway."

"When was he born?"

"The day you called."

He jerked toward her. "The day I called? But that was only eight months!"

"He was premature by a month. They kept him in the hospital for a week after I was discharged, but he's caught up now." She couldn't help the pride in her voice as she glanced down at the nursing baby. "The pediatrician says he's right where he should be for a two-month-old."

"Or you could be lying again, and he's somebody else's kid."

Her head snapped up. "How dare you imply such a thing?"

His harsh laugh made Bartholomew twitch in her arms, but she managed to quiet him again.

"You haven't given me much reason to trust you. Either you lied to me on the phone that day, or you're lying now. Which is it?"

She longed to tell him to take her back to the airport, but she kept thinking of Janice and little Clare. She had to withstand whatever Chase dished out, for Bartholomew's sake. "This baby is your son." She focused on

Bartholomew's contented face. "All you have to do is look at him to know that."

Chase met her statement with silence, then a shaky sigh. She glanced up to see him staring out the windshield again. His throat moved in a swallow and his voice sounded strained. "Why didn't you tell me?"

She mentally prepared herself, knowing this issue would be the most difficult. "Because no one knows about that night in the snowstorm, Chase. And I'd rather they didn't."

He didn't respond right away, and when he did, his tone was rough. "What'd you do, trick some other guy into thinking Bartholomew was his?"

She gasped and looked up. "I would never do that."

"Why, because it's dishonest?" Sarcasm dripped from each word.

She held on to her temper and met his look of disdain. "I've done what I thought best for all of us. Once you get over the first shock of finding out about Bartholomew, you'll see I was right."

"And what have you done, Amanda?"

"I told people—" She paused and cleared her throat. "I told people I'd gone to a sperm bank, that my biological clock was ticking and I'd decided not to wait for the right man to come along before I became a mother."

"Good God."

"It's for the best! We're from different worlds. I thought we settled that when you dropped me off at my apartment the next morning. A baby doesn't change that fact."

"The hell it doesn't! We were talking about whether to *date*. I don't remember giving up my rights as the father of our child."

Her throat felt tight as tears threatened. "Oh, Chase, you don't realize how my parents would react. I can't tell them that I . . ."

"Gave yourself to a disreputable trucker in the middle of a freak snowstorm?"

"That's not—"

"Yes, that's exactly what you mean." His green eyes flashed with something that looked like pain, and then his expression became hard. "And I can see that a woman like you would never admit to a one-night stand in the cab of a truck. What was I thinking?"

"You make me sound like a snob. I'm not."

His laugh was bitter, his tone suddenly coarse. "That night you weren't, lady. In fact, I really believed I had a full-blooded woman on my hands. Instead, I discover you're a cowardly little girl. But that's okay. You were still the best lay I've ever had."

Tears filled her eyes. "You're being crude on purpose."

"I'm a trucker, sweetheart. We're all crude. Haven't you heard that?"

She turned away from the taunt in his eyes. With her back to him she transferred Bartholomew to the other breast.

"So tell me." He ran a finger up her spine over the damp material of her thin cotton blouse and she shivered. "What brings you to Arizona? Got a hunger for some of that trucker loving?"

She fought down her rage so that she wouldn't frighten Bartholomew again. "If my hands were free, I'd slap your face for suggesting that," she snapped.

"That isn't the reason you flew all the way out here? Shucks, I'm just a dumb trucker, so I can't imagine any other reason. You don't need money, and you don't want my name. What else could you be after besides my body?"

"*Will you stop that?*" she hissed.

"Listen, Ms. Drake, and listen good. You've just stepped off that plane with my baby and announced that everyone thinks his daddy is some sperm-bank donor. You just lost the right to dictate to me! Now tell me what you came for and save us both some time. Then I can put you on the next plane to New York and get on with my life."

She shuddered. If she'd thought he would react in the easy, civilized way her other male friends might have, she'd sadly miscalculated. In her heart she'd known what to expect, though. A man who could love with such thoroughness could hate just as thoroughly. She kept her back to him and took a deep breath. "I need to know something about your family's medical history. An incident with a friend of mine convinced me that's it's irresponsible of me to raise Bartholomew without knowing if he's genetically predisposed to any life-threatening diseases."

"I'm surprised you didn't send me a form to fill out."

She'd thought of it. "I was afraid you'd ignore a form." Or barrel back to New York and confront her. "Also it seemed a little . . . cold."

"Really? So instead, you traipse out here, dangle my son in front of me while you get your information and whisk him away again. You're all heart, Amanda."

Amanda gritted her teeth and prayed for the strength to get the information she needed without killing the man who possessed it. "I've tried to handle this so that it's best for all of us. Someday you might even realize that."

"I assume you didn't tell anyone the real reason you decided to come out to Arizona, then," he said.

"I said I needed a vacation and I'd heard good things about this guest ranch."

His dry laugh held no humor. "Your friends and family must be even dumber than I am to fall for that one. An Arizona ranch in July? With a baby?"

"I've always had a fascination with the West. My maternity leave isn't up for another two weeks, and the agency suggested I take a little trip. My mother thought I should go to Colorado instead, but I told her I wanted to see one of those giant cactus with the arms, like the one they have back at the airport." She remembered the name she'd been trying to think of. "Saguaros."

"You pronounce the name with a silent g," he corrected.

"Oh."

His voice gentled. "But I said it wrong when I first got here, too."

Bartholomew's tug at her nipple grew gradually weaker. Amanda eased him away from her breast and refastened her clothing before holding him against her shoulder and patting his back. Soon his burp came, loud as a bullfrog's mating call.

"My God, was that *him?*"

She glanced at Chase, a smile tugging at her mouth in spite of herself. "Are you suggesting it was me?"

Amusement flickered in his eyes. "He sounds like a trucker with a belly full of beer."

"He does, at that." The moment of shared delight took her breath away. She'd had no idea what she'd been missing. As tears welled up in her eyes again, she averted her gaze and rubbed Bartholomew's back until he relaxed into sleep. "Are you willing to give me the information I need?" she asked without looking at Chase.

There was no reply.

"I'm sure you're upset, but the medical background is really important. Just tell me if you know of any diseases I should watch out for."

Still no answer.

She glanced sideways and found him staring straight ahead, his arms draped over the steering wheel. She could read nothing from his expression. "There's a notebook in the outside pocket of the smaller of my two suitcases," she said. "If you'd be willing to get it and write down the information, you could take me back to the airport and I'll book a flight home. I can see that I shouldn't stay here any longer than necessary."

"Is there someone else?" he asked at last, without changing position.

"Someone . . . you mean another man in my life?" Her heartbeat quickened at the personal nature of the question, and the implication of his asking it. As furious as he must be, she was astonished that he'd want to know. "No. I haven't dated since I found out I was pregnant. Starting a relationship seemed an unnecessary complication."

He glanced over at her. "Did you mean it about wanting to see saguaros, or was that just another lie?"

"Dammit, I do not habitually lie," she said, hurt by the unexpected accusation. "I swear, if I didn't have a sleeping baby in my arms, I'd—"

"If you didn't have a sleeping baby in your arms, you wouldn't be here, would you?"

"No, I wouldn't," she admitted.

"My giving up trucking and investing in this ranch wouldn't have made any difference to you."

"Why would I start a relationship with a man in Arizona? I have a career based in Manhattan." She wondered why the explanation sounded restrictive today, when she usually took great comfort in the foothold she'd gained. "Besides, we have nothing in common, Chase. We established that ten months ago."

His glance flicked to Bartholomew.

"Okay, one thing."

He met her gaze with bold assessment in his eyes. "Oh, I think we have two things in common, Amanda. Even you can't deny that. We spent several hours proving it to ourselves."

She blushed. "Sex is not enough to base a relationship on. You know that as well as I do."

"I always figured it was a damn good start. But I wouldn't want to meddle with your prejudices."

Her heart thudded erratically as she tried to maintain her poise. Despite the joyful outcome of having Bartholomew, she'd been a fool to give in to her impulses that night in the storm and she mustn't let good judgment desert her again. She just needed her information and she'd be on her way back to her ordered life. "Don't worry about the notebook," she said. "Just tell me what you can. I have a good memory."

"I don't."

Her chest squeezed. "What do you mean?"

"I can't just spew this stuff out. I'll need some time to think, maybe check with a few people. So, did you want to see the saguaros or not?"

She could see where this was leading. "It's not important. I think it would be better if we ended our association as quickly as possible. A letter would be fine. Now that you know what I need, you can send a letter to the agency."

"Scared, Amanda?"

Her pulse raced. "Of what?"

His knowing smile, this time including his dimple, was the only answer required.

"Of course not!"

Chase opened his door. "Then let's strap the baby in the infant seat and start out to the ranch. Along the way, I'll show you a few saguaros."

3

BARTHOLOMEW SLEPT the entire ride to the ranch, leaving Amanda free to gawk at the unfamiliar countryside. And gawk she did. Used to the gentle slopes of the Adirondacks, she stared in amazement at the rough-hewn peaks of the Santa Catalina Mountains towering above Tucson. The route to the True Love curved around the backside of the range, and by the time Chase had guided the van onto a dirt road marked True Love Guest Ranch, Amanda had seen enough saguaros and other prickly plants to last her a lifetime. She had the urge to encase Bartholomew in a suit of armor to protect his soft baby skin from the bristling terrain.

Chase drove in silence, his expression as austere as the landscape. If she didn't so desperately want the information about his family, she'd consider calling a cab when she arrived at the ranch and returning to the airport. His question about whether there were any other men in her life made her wonder if he had ideas of renewing their sexual relationship. If so, he'd be disappointed—she had no intention of letting that happen. Or maybe he just wanted a little more time with Bartholomew. She could hardly deny him that, considering her request for his medical background, but she hoped he wouldn't become too attached to the baby.

The van jounced over a pothole in the dirt road and Chase muttered a curse under his breath.

"Is it your back?" she asked, recalling belatedly that a couple of months ago he'd been in a hospital bed.

"No. I didn't want to wake the baby," he said.

She was unexpectedly touched. "Don't worry. He'll probably sleep until the van stops. How is your back?"

"Not bad."

She decided to press the point. "But you gave up your truck-driving career because of your back, didn't you?"

He nodded. "The physical therapists said it would be at least a year before I could get through a day without pain, and the doctors doubted I'd ever go back to trucking. But I've had a sort of miracle cure out here. Four weeks ago, I started riding, and now, on a good day, I can stay in the saddle for several hours."

It wasn't hard to picture him galloping through this rugged country. The role suited him in the same way driving a powerful 18-wheeler had, and both images stirred her sexually. But she'd already indulged herself in the fantasy once, and the price had been high. Indulging again could threaten her whole way of life. "I imagine the climate would help a bad back." She lifted her hair to let the air-conditioning find the nape of her neck.

He glanced at her, and his gaze warmed. She remembered too late that he'd once commented on that gesture, calling it "damn sexy." Self-conscious, she released the weight of her hair to her shoulders. She hadn't meant to be provocative. She didn't want him to want her.

"The warm weather helps," Chase said after a moment. "And the head wrangler, Leigh Singleton, well, she has some amazing massage techniques."

"Oh." The jolt of jealousy that hit Amanda caught her completely off guard. She had no right to those kinds of emotions. And they were a dangerous sign that she might have been fooling herself about why she'd come to Ari-

zona. "You're lucky to have found someone like that," she
said.

"Leigh is a fascinating woman. I never believed in
psychics or natural healing before, but Leigh's changing
my mind."

Amanda didn't trust herself to speak. It was one thing
for her to decide their relationship had no chance. It was
quite another to hear Chase praising the "fascinating"
attributes of another woman. Yet she could hardly expect a man with Chase's sex appeal to remain without a
woman for very long.

"Well, here we are," Chase said, pulling the van to a
stop.

Amanda had a brief glimpse of a low wall that arched
over a wrought-iron gate. Behind the wall was a large
one-story structure of whitewashed adobe with a red-
tiled roof and a wide front porch splashed with red ge-
raniums in pots.

Bartholomew started to whimper in the seat behind
her, cutting short her inspection.

"I'll get him," she said, opening her door. By the time
she'd extricated Bartholomew from his infant seat, Chase
was already striding down the flagstone walk carrying
her luggage. Leaving the van door open, she followed
him.

The lightweight designer blouse and skirt she'd chosen for the trip had seemed sensible enough at the airport, but now she could see they belonged at a beach
cottage, not a ranch. Her open-toed sandals collected dirt
and small stones that bit into the soles of her feet and
threatened to destroy her nylons.

Shielding Bartholomew from the relentless sun, she
hobbled up the walk toward the porch, where an old
cowboy sat in a cane chair with a black-and-white dog

at his feet. Except for the aluminum walker beside him, the old man looked like something out of a Norman Rockwell painting. Amanda could imagine using him as part of an ad campaign for the True Love, and automatically began composing copy to describe the timeless appeal of a shady porch on a summer afternoon.

Chase set the luggage down on the porch and touched the brim of his hat. "Afternoon, Dex."

The gesture of respect charmed Amanda more than she cared to admit. She remembered the crudeness with which he'd described her as "the best lay he'd ever had," and wondered which was the real Chase, the rough-edged trucker or the gallant cowboy.

"Who's this?" the old man asked with disarming bluntness.

"I'd like you to meet Amanda Drake," Chase said, turning toward her. "And . . . her son," he added, glancing away.

"Your girl?"

"No, she's . . . someone I knew in New York. Amanda, this is Dexter Grimes. He used to be foreman of the True Love."

Amanda stepped onto the porch where the shade enveloped her in coolness. She shifted Bartholomew to the crook of her left arm and held out her right hand. "Glad to meet you, Mr. Grimes."

"Likewise." He gripped her hand firmly just as Bartholomew began to fuss.

"Excuse me." She extracted her hand and began to jiggle the baby against her shoulder. "He's had a long trip."

Dexter held out his arms. "Here."

She stared at the old cowboy. Relinquish her precious baby to a man so uncoordinated he needed a walker to get around? "That's okay, Mr. Grimes. I'd better just take him inside."

Dexter lowered his arms, his gaze sad. "Too old."

"Oh, no!" Sympathy washed over her. "I just . . ." She glanced at Chase for help, but he returned her gaze without saying a word. Slowly, she turned back to Dexter. Mentally crossing her fingers, she leaned over to offer him her squirming child. "He's a handful," she said cautiously, lowering Bartholomew into Dexter's arms.

"Yep." Dexter cradled the baby as if he'd been holding children for years, and an expression of delight spread over his leathery features. Bartholomew stopped fussing and stared up at the old man. "Pretty," Dexter said.

Amanda's eyes misted. She hadn't received such an uncomplicated expression of joy from either of her own parents. "Yes, he's very pretty," she said.

"Stinks some," Dexter said.

Amanda's chuckle mixed with the lump of emotion in her throat. "I think he needs a change."

Dexter laughed softly as he looked down at the baby. "Could be." He brushed a finger under the tiny chin. "Could be."

And then something happened that took Amanda's breath away. Bartholomew grasped the old man's finger tight in one small fist, and smiled.

She grabbed Chase's arm. "Did you see that? Bartholomew smiled! Chase, he's never done that before. It's the first time!"

Chase glanced at her hand on his arm and she quickly removed it. "Guess he likes ol' Dex," Chase said easily.

"Likes me." Dexter played a gentle tug-of-war with the baby.

Behind them the carved double doors opened. Amanda turned at the creak of hinges and discovered a gray-haired woman with an ample bosom standing in the doorway. "What are you folks standing out in the heat for?" she asked in a lilting voice.

"Foal...no...little...baby!" Dexter said. "There! I said it! Baby!"

"What?" The woman circled Chase, the luggage and Amanda to stand in front of Dexter. "Sakes alive! It is a baby!"

"I said so."

Chase cleared his throat. "Belinda, this is Amanda Drake. Amanda, this is Belinda, Dexter's wife and the person who supervises the kitchen."

Belinda glanced quickly behind her with a smile and a nod. "Nice to meet you," she said before returning her attention to Bartholomew. "But who is this, Dexter?" She reached for the baby and Dexter handed him up to her.

"Baby," he said.

"I can *see* that." Belinda cradled Bartholomew in the crook of her arm and beamed down at him. "And a beautiful baby you are, too," she crooned. "Look at those big eyes! And such curly hair. And a cute little button nose, and rosy cheeks! You are a charmer, you are!"

Chase shifted his weight and hooked his thumbs through the loops of his belt. "That's Amanda's son." He coughed into his hand. "Bartholomew."

Amanda knew in that moment that Chase didn't like the name she'd chosen, and disappointment pricked her. Not that she should care if he liked the name or not, she told herself.

Belinda looked up at Chase. "Why, he looks just like *you*, Chase," she blurted out. Then she blushed. "Goodness, I probably shouldn't have said that."

"It's okay, Mrs. Grimes," Amanda said. "Chase is technically the father."

Chase spun toward her. "Technically? What kind of ridiculous statement is that?"

Heat rose in Amanda's cheeks. A moment ago, she'd been enjoying the response of these two sweet old people to her baby, almost as if she and Chase had brought Bartholomew home to adoring grandparents. Now the illusion was shattered. "Simply that I don't expect you to shoulder any of the responsibilities of being a father," she said.

Bartholomew, as if he were a barometer of the mood, began to cry.

"I need to take him in and change him," she said, holding out her arms toward Belinda.

"Of course." Belinda leaned down to drop a kiss on the baby's forehead before she gave him up. "He's so sweet."

"Stinks some," Dexter said.

"I'll just go inside and take care of that," Amanda said. "Mrs. Grimes, where would be a good place for me to change him?"

"Come with me. And call me Belinda." The older woman picked up the diaper bag, circled Amanda's waist with one arm and guided her toward the open door. Then she glanced over her shoulder. "Chase, take Amanda's luggage out to the cottage. I think we have an old cradle in storage. Get Rosa to help you find it and clean it up."

Amanda couldn't help smiling at Belinda's tone. She didn't speak to her boss as if she were an employee. Amanda suspected it had been many years since Belinda had felt like anyone's hired help.

They entered a high-ceilinged room that was blissfully cool.

"That was kind of you to let Dexter hold your baby," Belinda said. "Ever since his stroke, he's been so frustrated—can't always find the right word, can't move around as well as he used to. He was such a vital man. It's heartbreaking."

Amanda met the older woman's gaze. "I can imagine it would be," she said gently.

"He was delighted with that baby." She gave Bartholomew a wistful smile before gesturing toward a door to the right. "This way. We'll change him in Freddy's office."

Amanda surveyed the room as they started across it. Directly opposite the front door, a huge picture window revealed a landscaped patio with a pool and a Jacuzzi. A low wall swooped up to an arch, where a waterfall cascaded into the pool, transforming the surface of the water into dancing points of sunlight.

It would have been an idyllic setting except for the cowboy and cowgirl arguing heatedly beside the pool. Intrigued, Amanda paused. She couldn't tell what they were saying, but from the arm-waving and belligerent stances of both, she knew they were furious.

Belinda noticed Amanda's preoccupation. "Never mind them. They're in love."

"Doesn't look like it."

Belinda laughed. "It's been like that between those two ever since T. R. McGuinnes came to the ranch. Now, of course, we all call him Ry instead of T.R. That was the first thing Freddy did—got rid of those stupid initials and gave him a name you could say without laughing."

"Freddy's a woman?" Amanda had assumed the office they were heading for belonged to a man.

"I'm sorry. I forgot that you don't know who anybody is around here. Ry is one of the three owners of the ranch, and Freddy's the foreman. They're getting married in two days, so we don't have any regular paying guests staying here just now, only members of the wedding party. I guess that's why Freddy and Ry feel free to carry on like that by the pool. When we have paying guests, they usually save their spats for the corrals or the open range."

Just then, the dark-haired woman out on the patio pushed the broad-shouldered cowboy into the water.

"They're getting married?" Amanda jiggled Bartholomew on her shoulder to buy a little time so she could watch the exciting show outside. She'd never known anybody who acted this way, and she was fascinated. "But she just pushed him in the water, clothes and all!" The cowboy swam awkwardly to retrieve his floating hat while the woman stood back, arms crossed, and watched.

"They'll make up. Wait and see."

The woman named Freddy turned on her booted heel and marched, head down, toward the French door leading into the room where Belinda and Amanda stood. She opened the door and turned to shout over her shoulder. "They could rope me with barbed wire and drag me to the altar and I still wouldn't marry the likes of you!" Then she closed the door with enough force to rattle the panes. She obviously didn't notice she had an audience until she turned her attention away from the man still groping for his hat in the choppy water.

"Oh!" she said, her hand going to her throat. "Sorry about that."

"Freddy Singleton, meet Amanda Drake and her son," Belinda said. "I didn't catch the baby's name, Amanda."

Amanda lifted her chin. "Bartholomew."

"What a lovely name," Belinda said, earning Amanda's immediate loyalty.

"I'm pleased to meet you," Freddy said, coming forward with her hand extended.

Amanda barely managed to return the handshake as Bartholomew began wriggling and protesting. Amanda could read questions in Freddy's eyes, but the woman voiced none of them.

"We need your office as a place to change this little boy," Belinda said.

"That's fine." Freddy glanced out toward the pool as the cowboy hoisted himself out. "I think I'll be going now, anyway."

Belinda smiled. "I would, if I were you. I doubt if the water cooled him off any."

"He is so pigheaded!" Freddy said, edging toward the front door as a dripping Ry McGuinnes headed purposefully in her direction. "Well, see you later. Gotta run."

As she dashed out the front door, her wet fiancé entered through the back, his jaw rigid. "Freddy!" he called. Then he glanced over at Belinda and Amanda. "Afternoon, ladies." He tipped his hat, sending a stream of water to the tiled floor.

"Ry, this is Amanda Drake and her son, Bartholomew," Belinda said. "Amanda, this is Ry McGuinnes."

His intense blue eyes widened as he looked at the tiny baby squirming and squalling in her arms. He started to say something but closed his mouth again.

"We have to get this baby's diaper changed," Belinda said, turning Amanda toward an office off the main room. "And you'll need to dry off or get back outside. We can talk later."

"Sure." Ry touched the brim of his hat. "Nice to have met you, Ms. Drake."

Amanda followed Belinda toward the office. Behind her she heard the front door open and Ry bellow Freddy's name again. It didn't sound to her like the call of a lovestruck fool, but what did she know? She had obviously left the familiar world of Eastern manners and conventions for the wild, wild West.

AFTER BARTHOLOMEW had a clean diaper and a more pleasant disposition, Amanda felt ready to view her accommodations.

Belinda walked her over to the little cottage. Chloe, Dexter's black-and-white dog started to follow them, but Belinda ordered her back to the ranch house. "Did you bring any other kind of shoes?" she asked as Amanda struggled along the rutted road toward the cottage.

"They all have open toes, if that's what you mean," Amanda said. "I knew it would be hot, so sandals seemed like the obvious choice." She looked at Belinda's leather running shoes. "Apparently not."

"Out here you're better off in these or boots. But don't worry. I'll bet we can find something you can borrow. You should have seen Ry McGuinnes when he first got here. Polished wing tips, designer tie, the works. Freddy fixed him up in no time."

"I'll bet Chase didn't arrive in wing tips."

Belinda laughed. "No, he didn't. Looked like a catalog cowboy at first, but he broke in those new duds real fast. He's taken to ranch life like a duck to water, especially now that Leigh's put him on a program to keep his back limber and healthy."

Leigh again, Amanda thought sourly. And if Leigh looked anything like her sister Freddy, she'd be very attractive.

"In fact, Chase has become such a cowboy, I doubt he could be happy living back East now," Belinda said.

Amanda got the message. "Don't worry, I'm not here to drag him back there," she said.

"I'm very glad to hear that, because I think it would break his heart to have to choose between his obligation to you and his love of the ranch."

"As I've told Chase, he has no obligation to me or Bartholomew."

Belinda met the comment with silence broken only by the crunch of their shoes on the path and the drone of insects in the nearby bushes. "I see," she said after a moment.

Amanda expected a question about why she was here at all, but none came, and for that she gave Belinda credit.

As they neared the cottage, Amanda's artistic sense was aroused by the quaint adobe structure, whitewashed like the main house, with the same red-tiled roof and a miniature porch shaded by several gracefully arching trees. Two Adirondack chairs on the porch reminded Amanda of her parents' beach house and made her feel more at home.

"I didn't expect so many trees in the desert," she said to Belinda as they reached the porch.

"Many Easterners don't." Belinda mounted the single step to the porch and produced a ring of keys from the pocket of her cotton trousers. "The ones with the avocado-green trunks and branches that look like feather dusters are palo verde, and the ones with the gnarled black trunks and delicate leaves are mesquite. Out here we prize our trees, because we prize the shade."

"I can understand that." She was drenched in perspiration. "Is the cottage air-conditioned?"

"Oh, yes." Belinda opened the door and cool air poured out, beckoning Amanda inside. "And fortunately, Chase had the good sense to turn it on for you when he brought over your bags," she added, stepping inside and walking over to adjust a crooked window shade.

Amanda followed her in and closed the door of the one-room cottage. The high-beamed ceiling and white-washed walls gave it an open, airy look. Amanda's practiced eye noted genuine antique furnishings, and the comforter on the black walnut four-poster was trimmed in Battenburg lace. On a bedside table sat an imitation 1920s phone, and through the open bathroom door she glimpsed a clawfoot tub.

Belinda cleared her throat, and Amanda realized she expected a comment on the cottage. "It's lovely," she said, and meant it.

Belinda smiled. "Most think so, even the ones who've stayed at fancy hotels. We're proud of the True Love. Did Chase tell you that John Wayne used to stay at the ranch when he was filming in Old Tucson?"

"No, he didn't."

"Shame on that boy. Then he probably didn't tell you how the ranch got its name, either."

Amanda sank to the edge of the bed and hoped it wasn't a long story. Belinda had been so good to her, but she was very tired, and Bartholomew would want to nurse again soon. "No, he didn't."

"Thaddeus Singleton—he's the one who home-steaded the ranch in 1882—fell in love with a dance-hall girl and decided to marry her. Well, the proper ladies of Tucson thought it was scandalous and told him so. He married Clara anyway, and called the ranch the True Love, just to show those old busybodies. His brand is a heart with an arrow through it."

"I've seen that logo." Amanda was unwillingly drawn into the tale. "Did they live happily ever after?"

"Absolutely. Thaddeus built Clara a little adobe house, not much bigger than this cottage, over near what's now the north boundary of the ranch. He even burned that brand into the lintel above the door."

"How sweet."

"Up until six weeks ago, you could still see the ruins of it, but there was a stampede that leveled it. Freddy and Ry found the lintel, split in two, and Ry had it pieced together and framed. They're mounting it on an easel for the wedding ceremony out by the old homestead."

"The wedding's going to be outside?" Amanda had a tough time imagining it in this heat.

"Outside, and on horseback," Belinda said.

"Really!"

"It should be interesting, what with Ry's best man being a dude and all. He's a commodities trader from New York who says he can ride, but we've all heard that before."

To her surprise, Amanda discovered that she wanted to see that wedding, especially after witnessing the pool incident between this intriguing couple. But she probably wouldn't be around day after tomorrow.

Bartholomew began to wiggle and make squeaking sounds.

"Looks as if the little fellow wants something to eat, so I'll leave you alone," Belinda said. Then she glanced around and scowled. "I just noticed Chase doesn't have that cradle in here yet. I'll go ride herd on him and find out what he's doing with all his time."

Amanda started to rise to bid Belinda a proper goodbye.

"Sit down, sit down," Belinda said, waving her hand at Amanda. "You must be exhausted. I'll have that cradle over in a jiffy, and then you and the little one can take a nap before dinner. We eat at six. Will you be able to find your way back to the main house?"

"I'm sure I will. And thank you for all your help, Belinda."

Belinda cast a fond look at Bartholomew. "I didn't realize I was so eager to have a baby around. We don't accept guests with children that young, so I don't get much chance to see really little ones. They brighten up the place. I guess I'll have to start pestering Ry and Freddy about having one." She paused to gaze at Bartholomew again. "Well, I'd better go hunt down that Chase Lavette." With a smile, Belinda left, closing the door firmly behind her.

Still holding Bartholomew, Amanda propped pillows against the headboard of the bed and kicked off her shoes before she unbuttoned her blouse and allowed him to nurse. With a sigh, she relaxed against the soft pillows. Maybe it was exhaustion, as Belinda had suggested, but she felt more relaxed than she had in a long time. She hadn't realized keeping secrets could be so stressful. Here at the True Love her secret was out, and nobody had shunned her, which brought more relief than she could have imagined. Chase had been upset, but who could blame him?

Maybe all he needed was a little time to see that she'd done the right thing. Perhaps she wouldn't have to cut off all contact. As long as Chase planned to stay in Arizona, she could bring Bartholomew out here once in a while for visits and nobody back home would ever have to know the truth. Of course, that would depend upon Chase and what he'd agree to, but it seemed like an ideal situation. Eventually, she might even tell her friends and family about Chase, when time had softened the scandalous nature of her behavior in the cab of that big black truck.

She and Chase had produced such a beautiful baby that night, she thought, stroking Bartholomew's downy head as he suckled on her breast. Had she gone to a sperm bank as she'd told everyone, she couldn't have found a finer candidate to father her child. A memory of Chase floated up, not the angry Chase she'd dealt with today, but the daring man who'd dug through three feet of snow to free her from her car and had carried her, shivering and scared to death, back to his truck. She closed her eyes and felt the warmth of the truck, the warmth of his arms.

He hadn't kissed her then, or made any sexual advances. Once he'd settled her safely in the cab with a cup of coffee in her hands, he hadn't touched her except to rub her feet to make sure they weren't frost-bitten.

Then when he was convinced she was okay, he'd pulled the big truck onto the snowy road, determined to drive them both safely back to the city. They'd talked as he'd battled the treacherous road conditions for another hour, until finally he'd given up and pulled into a rest stop. That's when it had dawned on her that she was about to spend the night with this sexy truck driver, that prim and professional Amanda Drake had never had a one-night stand in her life and that it was an extremely tempting possibility.

Bartholomew's suckling grew less vigorous and she eased him away from her breast. It didn't look as if Chase would arrive with the cradle in time for the baby's nap, and she didn't trust putting him on the bed now that he'd begun to roll. Lifting him in her arms and reaching for a diaper to protect her shoulder, she climbed off the bed and studied the room while she burped him.

The floor would do, she decided, pulling the comforter off the bed and folding it awkwardly with one hand. Finally, she'd created a soft padded surface that would cushion Bartholomew as he slept. A nap would be nice for both of them, she thought with a sigh as she settled him on the comforter.

On her hands and knees, she was stroking his back when a movement from the bedskirt caught her eye.

The bedskirt, also made of Battenburg lace, fluttered gently. She wondered if a draft from the air conditioner had caused it. The lace fluttered again. But there is no breeze down here, she thought, her heart pounding, her hand reaching for Bartholomew.

From beneath the lace darted a forked tongue.

4

AFTER NEARLY a half hour of looking, Chase and Rosa found the cradle behind boxes of Christmas decorations in a little-used storeroom. With a dustcloth Rosa gave him, Chase cleaned the cobwebs from it and in the process noticed the handholds carved into the headboard and footboard were in the shape of a heart. He wiped the dust from the handholds with care.

Rosa returned with a clean quilt that she folded into a serviceable mattress. After thanking her, Chase picked up the cradle, his fingers fitting perfectly into the hearts on either end, and started for the cottage. Carrying a cradle wasn't how he'd pictured this little trip to visit Amanda, he thought with a grimace. Now the scenes he'd imagined taking place in the cottage weren't likely to happen, unless he'd completely misread the signals she'd been giving him.

About a hundred yards from the cottage he heard a screech. He dropped the cradle and started forward just as the door flew open and Amanda bolted out, barefoot, with her blouse undone and Bartholomew clutched against one shoulder, screaming lustily.

"Snake!" she cried above the sound of Bartholomew's screams. She ran toward him, her eyes wide, her face the color of snow.

His blood froze in his veins. "Where?"

"Under...under the bed!"

He tasted the metallic flavor of fear. "Did it bite you?" He reached for the wailing child. "Is the baby—"

"No!" She stepped out of reach. "We're not bitten! Get it out, Chase! Just get it out!"

He glanced around for a stick and broke a forked one off a palo verde. "Stay there."

"Don't worry." She gasped for breath. "I'm never going back in that place."

He approached the door of the cottage with caution and listened, trying to tune out the baby's crying. Rattlers didn't always rattle, he'd learned, but if he heard the buzzing sound first, at least he'd have a better idea what he was dealing with. The cottage was silent. He knocked the stick against the open door. He heard nothing but the baby's ratcheting complaint.

With slow, even steps he walked through the door and cast a look over the polished oak boards covered with Indian-patterned throw rugs. On the far side of the room a white comforter lay folded on the floor, an indentation in the middle where the baby had obviously been lying. He shuddered. Amanda should have put him in the bathtub, but then, she didn't know. A New York copywriter would have no experience with snakes.

Not that a snake was even supposed to be in here. A maid had cleaned the room just that morning. He wondered if the reptile could have slipped through the door when he'd brought Amanda's suitcases over earlier, but he doubted it. He might be a little distracted by Amanda and the baby's arrival, but not *that* distracted.

Since the snake wasn't coming out to greet him, he supposed he'd have to search for it. Too bad it was probably hiding under the bed. He didn't relish putting his face down there at striking level to find out whether or not it was a rattler. Using the stick to lift the bedskirt at the foot of the four-poster, he hunkered down and peered into the shadows. His gut tightened. There was something under there, all right. Something big. He sure wished he had a flashlight.

Bartholomew's crying lessened, then stopped. Chase didn't like the idea of the little guy's being out in the sun too much longer. Time to get the damn snake out from under the bed. He rounded to the side, lifted the skirt with one hand and began to poke the thick body. If it was a rattler, it might come charging out at him. Despite the air conditioner blasting through the cottage, he began to sweat as he poised on the balls of his feet, ready to react.

With a dry whispering sound the snake began to uncoil. He waited, heart pounding, to see which side it would choose. It started moving away from him. Chase eased onto the mattress and inched to the other side, the forked stick poised. The shape of the head would tell him everything, but he hadn't been able to see it in the murky light sifting under the bedskirt. He held his breath.

The bedskirt moved, and the snake started out, its body thick as a baseball bat. Chase shoved the stick down hard just behind the creature's head, which was oval, not triangular like a rattler's. The intruder was a very large, very harmless, bull snake.

Weak with relief, he had a hard time holding the stick steady. Fortunately, the snake had become as motionless as a length of cable, as if complete stillness would keep it safe. It was several seconds before Chase gathered the coordination to reach down and grasp the snake behind the head where his stick had kept it pinned.

He wriggled off the bed and hauled the snake up. Chase was nearly six feet tall, and he had to hold the snake head-high before its tail no longer touched the oak floor.

"I have the snake, Amanda," he called out the door. "It's big, but it's harmless. I'm coming out. Don't be scared. It won't hurt you."

"You mean it's still *alive?*"

"You shouldn't kill them," Chase said, walking toward the door as the snake undulated in the air. "They help keep things in balance around here."

As he walked out on the porch, she gasped and stumbled backward, nearly running into Chloe, Dexter's dog poised right behind her. Chloe's ears pricked forward and she gave a sharp bark.

"Careful," Chase warned. The upended cradle lay a few feet beyond where she stood. "You could trip over the dog, and if you fall, there's a lot of prickly stuff you could land in."

"Of course there is. *Everything* around here is dangerous. I'm in the middle of 'Wild Kingdom'!"

Chloe wagged her tail and sat down next to Amanda. Chase could have sworn the dog, a golden retriever and sheepdog mix, had decided to guard Amanda and the baby.

"Maybe you'd better go back inside while I take this guy out and let him go," he said.

"Oh, God. You're letting it go?"

"I'll walk pretty far out." Chase stepped off the porch and Amanda backed up another step, nearly landing on Chloe's tail. "Besides, this fellow attacks rodents, not people. This snake is no threat to you or the baby. I promise. Now go on inside and wait for me. I'll be back real soon."

She shook her head.

He controlled his irritation. "Amanda, it's safe now, and the baby should be out of the sun. Chloe will react if there's anything else in there to be afraid of."

"I won't go in, and stop calling him *the baby!* If you can call a dog by her name, you can call him by his name, which is Bartholomew!"

God, how she tested his patience. "But I didn't get any say in that choice, did I?"

"And you hate his name." Her lips quivered as her gaze remained riveted on the snake he held aloft.

"No, I don't hate it. I just—aw, hell, Amanda. It's hot and I'm holding a very athletic snake. Can we discuss this later?"

"Just get that thing out of here," she said, her voice strained.

"You should go inside."

"No."

She looked pretty close to hysteria, so he decided not to insist. "Okay. You and . . . Bartholomew wait here. Chloe, stay with Amanda." The dog wagged her tail in response.

Chase started off through the desert as quickly as he could walk, considering he was wearing boots, avoiding cactus and carrying a six-foot snake that very much wanted to be loose. "Take it easy," he told the snake. "You were probably more scared than she was." Although he doubted it. Amanda had been pretty freaked-out.

She was right about his reaction to the baby's name. He didn't like it. Maybe that was because he'd had no say in naming the kid, but more than that, he thought "Bartholomew" sounded too long and involved for the kind of son he'd like to have, a sturdy little boy who lived to run and throw balls and eat ice cream. A kid who—

Chase brought his imagination to a halt. Where had all that come from? He'd never wanted a kid. Or had never admitted it. But then Amanda had arrived with his son, and unexpected dreams were surfacing. Dreams of a family. For all the good those dreams would do him. Just as Amanda hadn't given him any say in naming the baby, she hadn't invited him to help raise the boy, either. He'd have to fight for that right, and he didn't like the idea of what that might do to Bartholomew.

About two hundred yards from the cottage, he figured he could set the snake free. He lowered it slowly to the ground, released the head last and stepped away. In five seconds the snake was gone, taking off through the creosote bushes. Chase turned and hurried back to where Amanda still stood in the path, Chloe stationed right beside her.

"Where did it go?" she asked.

He tried a smile out on her. "Packed a bag and lit out for Texas."

"Don't try to joke about it. That snake was headed straight for Bartholomew."

"I guess I would have jumped out of my skin myself if I'd been there," he said, softening his tone. "Now let's get him back inside."

"Not until you check everything in the cottage." Her blue eyes still reflected full-scale panic.

"Then at least wait up on the porch in the shade," he said, taking her elbow.

She was stiff, but she allowed him to guide her to the porch. Chloe followed right beside her, panting loudly in the heat. "I don't belong here," Amanda said. "I want you to give me your medical history now, so I can take a flight out. Maybe I can even leave tonight."

"We'll talk about it in a minute." His first concern was getting them all into a cool environment. He left Amanda and the baby on the porch and took Chloe with him into the cottage. "Check it out, girl," he said, and Chloe seemed to understand, because she circled the perimeter of the room and sniffed every corner. Then she snuffled under the bed, obviously still smelling traces of the snake. Chase scoured every nook and cranny, including a closet, all the dresser drawers and a cupboard in the bathroom. He found only one small spider, a harmless kind, which he captured and tossed out the door as he came back to the porch.

"All clear," he said.

She entered slowly, her gaze sweeping the room several times.

"I'll get the cradle," Chase said. "I hope I didn't break it."

"It doesn't matter. I'm not staying."

Chase went after the cradle, anyway. He sincerely hoped he hadn't broken it when he'd dropped it. It had probably been built for a Singleton baby somewhere back in time, and he'd bet both Freddy and Leigh had been rocked to sleep in it. For a reason he didn't want to explore too thoroughly, he wanted Bartholomew to sleep in it, too. And he hoped Amanda wouldn't take the next plane out of town. Not because he wanted anything more to do with her, but because he couldn't say goodbye to his son just yet. Maybe in a few days he'd have it all worked out in his mind, but for now, he wanted that baby around.

The cradle was still in one piece, but the quilt had fallen in the dirt. He shook it out and tucked it under his arm. He'd noticed an extra blanket in the closet that he could use instead. Tossing the quilt on one of the porch chairs as he walked by, he carried the cradle into the room and shut the door behind him.

Amanda stood by the table jiggling Bartholomew against her shoulder as she stared out the window. "I'm sorry I blew up, but I want to go home, Chase," she said softly. "This isn't my type of place. Will you help me get back?"

"Not yet."

She looked up at him, rebellion flickering in her eyes. "I can just call a cab. I haven't even unpacked."

"I thought you needed information before you left."

"Maybe it's best if we communicate by phone."

His gut twisted. She could leave, and he had no power to stop her. He swallowed. "Please don't leave yet."

She studied him for several moments. "Chase, a snowstorm brought us together," she said finally. "Otherwise, we'd never have met because our lives were so different. They still are, even more so now that you're out here. Give me what I need and let me go. It's the best thing we can do with a situation we didn't ask for."

He struggled with the urges coursing through him. He'd never felt possessive about a woman in his life. Easy come, easy go had been a motto that had served him well for years. Yet he couldn't imagine watching Amanda walk out of his life. She was the mother of his child. That created a bond he couldn't take lightly. A shrink would probably say it was because in his own case, that bond had been so carelessly broken. At any rate, apparently Amanda didn't feel connected to him; she could hardly wait to get away from the True Love.

"I told you, I'm not very good at remembering things," he said. "I need to make some phone calls before I can give you what you've asked for. I haven't had a chance to do that yet."

"Can you do it now?"

"Maybe." Once he figured out where to start. He'd been out of touch for so long, he might find only dead-end streets. "I'll make some calls, Amanda, but I can't promise I'll get you quick results. If you really want to fly out now, I could mail you something, but I'm lousy at writing stuff out. I'd probably miss some detail you'd want."

She heaved a long, shaky sigh. "You're right. It's late, and we're both tired, and Bartholomew's been through enough for one day. I should at least stay until tomorrow, but . . ." She raised her eyes to his. "That snake frightened the daylights out of me, Chase. I don't know if I can sleep in this cottage tonight."

He almost offered to stay with her, but he thought she might misunderstand the offer. Maybe he didn't even mean it so innocently. Scared as he'd been when she ran out the door and shouted the word *snake*, he'd still noticed her unbuttoned blouse and had glimpsed her bare breast. Sometime during the incident, she'd refastened her blouse, but that didn't eliminate the air of sensuality that still clung to her like morning dew on clover. He might not love her, but he definitely lusted after her. "I'll bet Dexter would let you have Chloe for the night," he suggested.

At the mention of her name, Chloe sat between them and looked up, her tail thumping the floor.

Amanda gazed doubtfully at her. "I've never had a dog."

"Neither have I. But that doesn't matter. Chloe doesn't think she's a dog."

"She really knows when something's wrong?"

"Why do you think she came dashing down here? She heard you scream."

"Really?" Amanda reached down with her free hand and touched the dog's head. "Did you come to help me, Chloe?"

Chloe whined and thumped her tail faster.

"That's amazing. She doesn't even know me."

"I think it has something to do with the way Dexter reacted when you handed him Bartholomew. Chloe was watching all that, and I think she decided that he would be her responsibility, too."

Amanda fondled Chloe's head and scratched behind the dog's ears without looking at Chase.

When Chase heard a sniff, he guessed Amanda was crying. "Amanda?"

"Don't mind me," she said, her voice choked. She sniffed again. "I hear new mothers are sometimes emotional."

Chase had never met a crying woman he hadn't tried to comfort. He drew Amanda, baby and all, into his arms, careful to accommodate Bartholomew as he guided Amanda's head to his shoulder. She began to sob softly, her tears seeping through his shirt. Chase laid his cheek against her wondrous red hair and massaged the small of her back.

He wasn't being smart, he thought, but needy people always got to him. And Amanda had seemed that way from the beginning. Beneath the career-woman image, he'd sensed a hunger very much like his own. She might have thought all they shared in the cab of his truck that night was sex, but he'd always suspected it went much deeper than that.

Before they'd made love, she'd announced that she considered it a one-night stand, and he'd gone along with the idea. He hadn't been about to turn away from a woman as tempting as Amanda, and he'd been curious, too, wondering what it would be like making love to a woman who dressed in cashmere and drove a Mercedes. Soon, however, he'd forgotten everything about her except the light in her eyes and warmth of her body.

In the morning as they'd driven into the city, he'd made the mistake of asking when he could see her again. That's when he'd discovered that she really did consider him a one-night stand. Oh, she was grateful he'd saved her from the snowbank, and she'd had a terrific time—her exact words—but she didn't think they were at all suited to each other. His pride had made him agree with her. Yet he'd always thought she would reconsider, once the effects of that night had sunk in. She might have, he thought, if she hadn't been pregnant. Had he sensed all along that's what had happened? Probably.

She stopped crying and leaned weakly against his shoulder. Bartholomew had remained quiet the whole time, as if subdued by his mother's tears.

"I'm sorry, Chase," she murmured thickly.

"For what?"

"Everything." She sighed. "Just everything. I've tried to do what was best, but I didn't know that would be so hard on everyone."

"I wish you'd have let me help."

"I don't believe in saddling people with unwanted obligations."

"Amanda, I—"

"People hate obligations!"

His hand stilled in the act of rubbing her back. "Maybe I wouldn't think of it like that."

She lifted her head and met his gaze. "I'm not taking the chance that you would," she said with a vehemence that surprised him. "When I was sixteen, I worked part-time in my dad's law office and I overheard him telling his secretary he couldn't get a divorce because of his *obligation* to his wife and children. *I* was the reason he couldn't be happy, the reason he turned into a martyr who couldn't love anyone! Bartholomew's never going to have that feeling if I can help it."

Chase was silent. To be truthful, he wasn't sure how he would have reacted if she'd begged him to marry her and be a proper father to their child. Maybe like a martyr, just as she'd said. Marriage had never figured into his plans. But that didn't mean he wanted to be kept away from his baby, either. What, exactly, did he want? He wasn't sure. He'd trained himself not to want much of anything from life so that he was seldom disappointed.

But he was a father now. He couldn't drift along and take whatever came his way this time, or he'd lose contact with his son. He needed a plan, but clearheaded planning was difficult while he held Amanda in his arms. Her body pressed against his, the scent of that expensive cologne she wore and the memory of their shared night in the truck cab were working on his imagination. For the first few weeks after the elevator accident, he'd been in too much pain to think about sex, but his back didn't bother him much now. He'd been dreaming of this woman for ten months, and after her letter had arrived, he'd fantasized with great pleasure about undressing her again and making love to her in the antique four-poster bed next to where they now stood.

Slowly he released her and stepped back. She looked at him through reddened eyes. He supposed he should have been turned off by her puffy, tear-streaked face. Instead, he wanted to tuck the baby in the cradle and tuck her into bed, with him right alongside her. She had the fullest, most kissable mouth he'd ever seen, and it was parted now, just wide enough to allow his tongue to slip inside. There was an awareness in her eyes, a vulnerability that he recognized from that night in the truck.

"There's a blanket in the closet. You can use it as a mattress for the cradle," he said.

"All right." She didn't move, just kept holding the baby against her shoulder like a shield against the emotion shining in her eyes.

"You *are* afraid of me, aren't you?"

She swallowed. "Of course not."

"Then get the blanket and put the baby down."

Still she didn't move.

Muttering a soft oath, he looked away. "We're more alike than you think, Amanda. Neither one of us knows what to do about this problem. The difference is that I'll admit it." He started for the door, then glanced back at the dog sitting attentively beside Amanda. "I'll tell Dexter you're borrowing Chloe for a while." Then he stepped into the hot sunshine and quickly walked away from the little cottage while he could still resist the seductive light in those blue eyes. He wondered if she realized it was there.

SHE HADN'T EXPECTED to want him so much, Amanda thought as she took a deep breath and turned away from the door. She found the blanket he'd mentioned and arranged it in the cradle with one hand, not willing to put Bartholomew on the floor for even an instant.

She certainly remembered Chase as a very appealing guy, but she'd always thought his sexual magnetism had been heightened by the novelty of making love in the bunk of an 18-wheeler. Apparently, that hadn't been the secret of Chase's attraction for her. Once she'd sobbed out her frustration in his arms just now, she'd become aware of his strong arms wrapped around her. Very aware. Had she not been holding Bartholomew.... But she had been, and that had helped her focus.

Chase had told her he was a rambler, a lone wolf, proud of the fact he had no strings to tie him down. He'd even had *The Drifter* stenciled on his truck cab as a general bulletin of the fact. She'd worked hard to create a secure niche with her job and her career-oriented friends. Her parents boasted about her all the time, just as they boasted about her brother, Jason, who was with the diplomatic corps in Spain. They'd boasted a little less about Bartholomew, but as her father had said, "At least you didn't link up with some bum just so you could be a mother."

Remembering that statement and her father's years of sacrifice out of "obligation," Amanda had resisted the urge to throw herself into Chase's arms again. Barely.

Lowering Bartholomew into the cradle, she sat on the edge of the bed and used her toe to rock him gently to sleep. Chloe settled down at the foot of the cradle and put her head on her paws.

When at last Bartholomew's eyes drifted closed, Amanda lay back on the bed. Chase had been right about having Chloe there. Amanda was able to relax, knowing the dog was on duty. But she couldn't sleep. Not when all she could think about was the way Chase had looked at her before he left, his smoky green eyes heavy with passion.

5

CHASE OPENED the back gate leading into the patio and stormed through, not sure where he was headed. He almost ran into Eb Whitlock, who was carrying a potted rosebush in each hand. Eb's ranch, the Rocking W, bordered the True Love on the north, and Freddy had asked him to give her away during the wedding ceremony.

"Hey, cowboy!" Eb said in his typical boisterous bellow. "Somebody set your tail on fire?"

Chase wasn't in the mood for Eb Whitlock's corny brand of humor. The rancher usually laughed at his own jokes, and when he displayed his choppers, Chase was reminded of the grille work on his Peterbilt. "Didn't mean to run you down, Eb," he said. "I guess we're all rushing around these days, with the wedding coming up."

"Exactly. That's why I'm here with these." Eb plopped a container on either side of him, took off his hat and reached for a bandanna in his hip pocket. "Saw them in a nursery in town and couldn't resist." He mopped his forehead and smoothed the sides of his white hair before replacing the bandanna and repositioning his hat. "I have six more out in the truck. Thought they'd look good for the reception. Belinda said to find a place for them out here around the pool." He walked over by the waterfall. "Maybe one here. What do you think?"

Chase had to admit the roses were a nice thought, although it was typical of Eb to act on his own, without consulting anyone, when he wanted to do something generous. More than once, Chase had heard Ry mutter that he wished Eb would mind his own damn business.

"I don't know the first thing about flower arranging," Chase said, starting to edge away.

"Me neither. I'm just an old cowpoke trying to do a good deed." Eb walked around behind the waterfall. "I'll just put one on the other side, here."

"Well, I'd better be going." Chase eased toward the house, determined to escape while he had the chance.

"Say," Eb called out from behind the waterfall, "how's that little gal of yours, the one that was coming in from New York?"

Chase definitely didn't want to discuss Amanda—or the baby—with Eb. "Well, she—"

"Chase!" Leigh called, bursting from the main room of the house. "What's this I hear about Amanda's . . . baby. Oh, hi, Eb. I didn't see you out here."

Thanks, Leigh. But he couldn't be angry with her. Not Leigh. When he'd first arrived at the True Love, he'd been attracted by her looks—dark blond hair and a face that reminded him of the Mona Lisa. To his surprise, he and Leigh had become friends instead of lovers. He trusted her, which made their relationship very special indeed.

"A baby?" Eb set the second potted bush on the other side of the waterfall and walked toward them with a grin big enough to eat New York. "Don't tell me you took a bite out of the Big Apple before you left?"

"To be honest with you, Eb, this was as much a surprise to me as it is to you," Chase said.

Eb clapped him on the shoulder. "Then I think it's time we had a talk, man to man. It's dangerous to be ignorant of the birds and the bees, son. Isn't that right, Leigh?"

Leigh's almond-colored gaze was contrite as she looked at Chase. "Oh, I think Chase understands the birds and the bees. In fact, I think he might have written the manual on the subject. Anyway, if you'll excuse us, Eb, I need Chase to help with some chores down at the corrals. Ry was supposed to do it, but he's not available."

Eb winked. "What's wrong, bridegroom jitters?"

"Oh, I hardly think that's the problem, Eb. Nice roses. Too bad Freddy's allergic to them."

"She is?"

"Something terrible. Maybe you can plant those over in your garden."

"But Belinda never said anything about Freddy being allergic."

"With all the food preparation for the reception and thinking about that little baby, Belinda's a basket case. Trust me, Eb. A few minutes with those roses and we'll be toasting Freddy, the red-nosed bride. Nice idea, though. Come on, Chase. We have work to do." She pulled him toward the French doors leading into the main room of the house. "Sorry about that," she said as soon as they were inside. "I didn't see his truck out front and he was hidden behind the waterfall."

"Don't sweat it. Knowing Whitlock's sources, he'd have found out by sundown, anyway. Is Freddy really allergic to roses?"

"Not yet, but she will be if Ry finds out who trundled them over here unannounced. Their big fight this morning was over whether to have Eb in the ceremony. Ry doesn't want him."

"I don't blame him. Whitlock reminds me of a few truck drivers I've known—big belly and big mouth to match." Chase also knew that Eb had been an unsuccessful bidder for the True Love and hadn't taken well to defeat when Ry had closed the deal.

"The problem is, Freddy promised our father before he died that she'd ask Eb to walk her down the aisle if she ever got married. I think it was a dumb promise, but Freddy will never go back on it."

Chase glanced back at Whitlock, who had retrieved the rosebushes and was walking toward the door. "Let's get out of here." He took Leigh's elbow and they headed out the front door toward her truck. "By now, he's probably thought of a dozen questions about this baby business."

"I'll bet he heard a rumor about the baby and bought the roses so he'd have an excuse to come over and check it out. I'm getting mighty sick of the way Eb uses his little favors and gifts as a manipulation." She gestured toward the passenger door of her truck. "Hop in. You look like a man who could use some therapeutic shoveling."

"You read my mind, as usual." Chase climbed into Leigh's dark blue truck with the rainbow painted on the fender and a crystal hanging from the rearview mirror, which cast more rainbows around the interior. Leigh was one of the few people he allowed to drive him anywhere.

"I'll bet you've missed your swim today," Leigh said as she started down the road.

"I'll get it in tonight," Chase promised. He wasn't about to skimp on the rehabilitation program she'd set up for him, no matter what Amanda threw at him.

"Stress can zap those muscles, you know."

Chase leaned back against the tattered seat. "What makes you think I'm stressed?"

"Who wouldn't be? I doubt it's every day you have women show up with babies they claim you fathered."

"I did father this one, Leigh."

"I know. Belinda says he looks just like you." Leigh shifted into third gear. "But I can't understand what Amanda is doing out here if she doesn't want you to pay child support or anything."

"She wants information on my family's medical background."

Leigh looked skeptical. "She could have asked you that on the phone."

"And I might have hung up on her. Can you imagine getting a phone call like that?"

"I suppose you have a point, but she should have warned you."

"Yeah, she should have."

Leigh swerved to avoid a rabbit. "Something else is going on here, Chase. My intuition lights are flashing like crazy."

"Well, if you figure it out, tell me." They arrived at the corrals and Chase reached for the door handle. "In the meantime, I have some serious shoveling to do."

"Nothing like cleaning out a corral or two to lower the stress level." Leigh smiled. "Ry thinks we should bill it that way and charge the dudes a fee for the privilege of shoveling."

Chase laughed as he climbed from the truck, but he had to admit it was a good idea. "Are you joining me?"

"I'm not stressed. Besides, I need to check on Penny Lover."

"You're spoiling that mare," Chase said, rounding the truck and starting toward the tack shed.

Leigh was already on her way to a small corral at the far end of the clearing. "Expectant mothers deserve to be spoiled," she called back.

Chase silently agreed with her. And he hadn't been allowed to do that for Amanda, something else to add to his growing burden of regrets. He grabbed a shovel and rake from hooks on the tack-shed wall and headed toward the largest corral. He had the place pretty much to himself, except for the horses and the ever-present flies. Several of the hands had the day off, and there was no sign of Duane, the top hand, who was probably napping in the bunkhouse.

Chase raked and shoveled steadily for nearly thirty minutes, tossing manure into an open trailer used to haul it away. Finally, sweat-soaked and much calmer, he leaned against the shovel and took a breather. He loved being down here, surrounded by corrals built a century ago. They weren't the sort of corrals he'd expected when he'd pictured the ranch, though. Instead of open rails, the fences were made of gnarled mesquite branches stacked between upright supports to create a solid barrier. In Chase's opinion, they were part of what gave the True Love its own character, and he liked just looking at them.

Leigh walked over and leaned against the top of the fence. "Had enough?"

"I guess so. You ready to go back up to the house?"

Leigh nodded. "My maid-of-honor outfit needs a few finishing touches."

"Okay." Chase propped the rake and shovel against the side of the trailer and pulled off his gloves. "Let me wash off in the horse trough and I'll be right with you." Shoving the gloves into the back pocket of his jeans, he hung his hat on the rake handle and rolled up his sleeves.

"You're getting to be more of a cowboy every day," Leigh said. "A greenhorn wouldn't think of putting horse-trough water on his face."

"You'd better smile when you go comparing me to a greenhorn." Chase leaned over the trough and scooped water into his cupped hands. Splashing it over his face, he sighed at the welcome coolness.

Then his eyes began to burn. Seeking relief, he washed them with more water, but the burning grew worse. "Damn! My eyes!" he cried.

Leigh was over the fence and beside him in a flash. She cupped some water and stuck her tongue in. "Yuck!" She flung the water to the ground. "Something's wrong with this water! Go wash in the bunkhouse and send Duane out here. I'll keep the horses away from the trough."

Eyes streaming, Chase fumbled his way out the gate and ran toward the bunkhouse. "Duane!"

Duane opened the screen door and peered out. "What's wrong?"

"The horse trough is contaminated. Leigh needs help with the horses."

"Damnation," Duane muttered, and started toward the corrals at a bowlegged trot.

Chase caught the screen door before it slammed and barreled inside, his eyes stinging. He jogged the length of the barracks-like structure, deserted at this hour, to the bathroom at the end. After several applications of water from the sink's faucet, his eyes felt a little better. Grabbing a towel, he mopped his face and headed back outside.

By the time he'd returned to the corrals, all the horse troughs were draining. Duane was mounted on Destiny, the ranch's premier cutting horse, keeping the horses in the biggest corral away from the trough. Leigh was managing to distract the few horses in the smaller corrals.

"We'll need to get Freddy down here to check all the horses," Leigh called out to him as she maneuvered two geldings away from a draining trough. "Dammit! What could be in the water?"

"What about a sample?" Chase asked.

"Oh, God, yes! There should be a jar in the tack shed. Scoop some water out of that main trough before it's all gone."

Chase ran across the clearing, found an empty mason jar in the tack shed and managed to get back to the corral before the trough there was empty. He barely had time to get a sample of the water before the last of it drained into the mud.

"Did you get it?" Leigh hurried up beside him, with Duane close behind.

"Some, at least."

"Thank heavens you thought of it. When the horses are in danger, I really lose it." She pressed her fingers to her temples. "Let's see. We'll take the jar back up to the house, and Ry can run it into town to be analyzed while Freddy, you and I help Duane check the horses for any signs of poisoning."

"I thought Ry was unavailable."

She glanced at him, a suggestion of a smile easing the tension in her face. "He and Freddy had hung a Do Not Disturb sign on their door while they made up after their fight. But I think this warrants disturbing them." She turned to Duane. "Did you notice anything suspicious around the corrals today?"

Duane reached in his back pocket for his can of Red Man. "Nope."

"We're shorthanded this afternoon, so someone could have ridden in without being noticed."

Chase glanced at her. "Are you saying someone deliberately poisoned the water?"

"It's possible."

"Lots of things been happenin' around here." Duane stuck a plug of tobacco under his lower lip.

Uneasiness rolled in Chase's stomach. "Like what?"

"I'll tell you on the way back," Leigh said. "Let's get going."

"I'll drive."

She gave him another half smile. "Thanks, my trucker friend. I'd appreciate it this time."

"OKAY, let's have it," he said as they started down the road in her truck. "What's going on?"

"I was hoping it was over, but I guess not. Right before you three bought the ranch from the Colorado corporation, we were plagued with all sorts of accidents—leaking stock tanks, cattle tangled in barbed wire, stuff like that. Then there was that stampede the day you arrived. Freddy and Ry were almost killed."

"And we found out the gate had been accidentally left open. People make mistakes." Boy, did he ever know the truth of that one.

"Ry still thinks Duane might have had something to do with that stampede."

"You've got to be kidding!"

Leigh sighed. "I can't believe it, either. But I have to admit he might have a reason. He knows you guys are thinking about selling the ranch to developers. That would put an end to a way of life for Duane, not to mention screw up the breeding program he's conducting on the side, using True Love land. If the accidents drive you away, or at least devalue the property so you can't get a decent price, things might not change for him. And, after all, it was his herd that made up the stampede."

"But Duane wouldn't poison a horse trough."

"Well, Eb Whitlock is always another possibility. He still wants the ranch. And Ry even suspects Belinda."

Chase gave her a startled glance. "Belinda? Why in hell would he be suspicious of Belinda?"

"Because she's so protective of Dexter. Ry thinks she'd do anything to keep him sitting safely on that front porch. She hates the idea of your selling to developers. So do I, for that matter."

Chase fought panic. "But if we don't sell the ranch, we won't make the profit Ry told us about."

"Oh, come on, Chase! Do you mean to tell me you're still interested in getting rich? I've seen how you react to this place. You love it!"

He became aware of a hollow ache in the vicinity of his heart. "I've trained myself not to love any place too much."

Leigh was silent for a long moment. "That's the saddest thing I've ever heard you say," she murmured said at last.

DESPITE HER CONVICTION that she wouldn't sleep, Amanda eventually drifted off. She awoke feeling cozy, a remarkable feat considering the snake episode, she thought. Bartholomew remained asleep, and she enjoyed the luxury of washing her face and deciding what to wear to dinner without carrying a baby around while she did it. Chloe stayed at her post, merely lifting her head when Amanda walked past to open the suitcases.

She'd brought one pair of designer jeans and she decided on a white silk blouse that was tailored enough to be almost western in style. And she wouldn't make the mistake of wearing nylons with her sandals this time.

She barely made it through dressing before Bartholomew woke up, a little before six. He didn't seem particularly interested in nursing, so she changed him, put him in the infant seat and started out the door, with Chloe at her side. Then she paused. Beside the door sat a pair of boots, very nice brown leather boots, with a note tucked in the shank of one.

> Belinda said you might be able to use these and figured we were about the same size. You're welcome to borrow them during your stay.
>
> *Leigh Singleton.*

Amanda glanced from her open-toed sandals to the boots. Leigh's boots. Fantastic Leigh, who could read minds and had massaged Chase to health. Then Amanda gave herself a mental shake, feeling thoroughly ashamed of herself. Despite the fact she'd had Chase's baby, she'd relinquished all claim to him. What kind of woman discarded a man yet resented his attention to someone else? Amanda knew what kind, and it rhymed with witch.

She took the boots inside and changed out of her sandals. They were a perfect fit. As she walked to the main house with the boots lending her added height and Chloe trotting by her side, she almost felt as if she belonged at the True Love Ranch.

Retracing the path she'd taken with Belinda, she entered the patio through a back gate. Dexter sat in a shady corner across the pool, his walker by his side along with a dish of dog food. Chloe's head went up and her nose twitched. She glanced at Amanda.

"Go ahead," Amanda said. "I'll catch up with you later."

Chloe bounded toward Dexter, who greeted her with such affection that Amanda felt guilty about borrowing the dog for the night. But not guilty enough to refuse. Chloe would bring greater safety to Bartholomew, and that was Amanda's first priority. She waved at Dexter. "Thanks for loaning me your dog."

"Yep."

"Aren't you coming in to dinner?"

"Nope."

"Well, I'm starved," she said. "See you later."

"Yep."

The dining room was bustling, with Ry and Freddy at the center of all the activity. Amanda slipped in unnoticed and chose a table by herself, figuring the wedding guests, none of whom had brought children, would prefer not to have a baby around during their meal. She propped Bartholomew's infant seat on the chair next to her and gave her order to the young waiter who'd appeared.

Ry and Freddy had pushed three tables together to accommodate their crowd of well-wishers. Bartholomew dozed in his infant seat, so Amanda amused herself by figuring out who was who. The man who seemed to be an older version of Ry was definitely his father, but from body-language clues Amanda decided the woman with the elder McGuinnes wasn't Ry's mother. Ry was much more affectionate with another woman in her sixties, who sat with a different man. Divorced parents, Amanda concluded. After that, she had more trouble sorting out who might be friends, siblings or in-laws. Chase was nowhere around.

But Ry and Freddy had definitely made up. Wistfully, Amanda observed their affectionate interplay.

"How are the boots?"

Amanda turned to find a stunning blonde standing next to her table. Soft brown eyes with a hint of mystery complemented a face that would have delighted the Renaissance masters, Amanda concluded. "You must be Leigh." She stood and extended her hand. "Thanks for the boots. They fit as if they were made for me."

"How lucky." Leigh smiled and glanced over at Bartholomew. "Sweet baby."

On cue, Bartholomew began to fuss.

"He's probably hungry," Amanda said, reaching for him. "His timing leaves much to be desired."

"Since your dinner's not here, why don't you feed him?"

Amanda was taken aback. "Oh, I think this is too public a place. I can walk over to the cottage."

"Nonsense. Nursing is a natural part of life. If anyone's sensibilities are disturbed, that's their problem. Besides, if I sit here and screen you from view, nobody will even notice. Go ahead."

"Well . . . okay." Amanda hadn't yet nursed Bartholomew in a restaurant setting, and she felt self-conscious, but Leigh's comments made sense. As unobtrusively as possible, she unfastened the first few buttons of her blouse, unhooked the cup of her nursing bra, and guided Bartholomew to her nipple. She glanced at Leigh, who watched with a gentle smile. "Thank you for your understanding."

"If he's a typical little Taurus, food is very important to him."

Amanda laughed. "I read that. And so far it's really true. I'll have to make sure he doesn't turn into a little chub."

"I doubt he will. Neither you or his father—" Leigh paused. "Sorry. Maybe you'd rather I not talk about Chase."

"I'd . . . rather you did. I think I've handled the matter of Chase poorly. Maybe you can help me."

"I can try." Leigh glanced over Amanda's shoulder. "Excuse me a minute." She rose from her seat and intercepted the waiter who approached with Amanda's dinner. He headed back toward the kitchen. "I told him to keep it warm for five minutes."

"Thank you." Amanda decided Chase was a lucky man to have found someone as thoughtful as Leigh. She was determined to be happy for him, even though it hurt—unreasonable though that might be—to think of him making love to someone else.

Leigh resumed her seat. "First of all, what do you want from Chase?"

"Just his family's medical history, so I can be prepared for anything."

"That's all?"

"Absolutely, Leigh. Don't think I'm any threat to you. Once I have the information, I'll disappear with Bartholomew and—"

"Whoa! Back that pony up a minute. Threat to *me*?"

"Not that you're acting threatened," Amanda hurried on. "In fact, you're being far more generous than I would be in similar circumstances. I think Chase is very lucky to have someone like you."

Leigh grinned. "You think Chase and I are lovers, don't you?"

"You're not?"

"I know it's hard to believe, given that Chase is a very sexy-looking guy, but the chemistry isn't there between us. He's like the brother I never had, and to his great surprise, he thinks of me as a sister. Neither of us would dream of jeopardizing that."

"Oh."

"You should see the relieved look on your face, Amanda. Are you sure you came out here just for a medical history?"

Amanda looked away. Bartholomew seemed to be losing interest in nursing, so she nudged him away from her breast and concentrated on refastening her clothes. "It wouldn't work," she said finally, glancing up at Leigh. She placed a napkin over her shoulder and held Bartholomew there while she patted his back. "I've finally established myself in the New York advertising world. In my spare time I enjoy concerts and gallery openings, or discovering new ethnic restaurants. Can you picture Chase living that kind of life?"

"No."

"Then there's the extra psychological baggage of getting to know each other when a baby is already part of the equation. I don't think any relationship should begin under that kind of pressure."

"Probably not, but we live in an imperfect world." Leigh turned as the waiter arrived with Amanda's dinner. "Why don't you let me hold Bartholomew while you eat?"

Amanda tensed. "I couldn't impose on you like that. I can just put him in his seat."

"Where he may or may not want to stay. Let me take him. If you knew me better, you'd realize that I don't offer to do things I don't want to do."

Amanda gazed at her steaming plate of barbecued ribs and realized she'd need both hands if she intended to do the meal justice. And she was starving. "Okay. Bring him back if he's any trouble." She placed Bartholomew in Leigh's outstretched arms.

"Oh, we won't have any trouble, will we, Bartholomew?" Leigh smiled down at the baby. "Come and tell Auntie Leigh all your secrets."

Amanda watched in wonder, and more than a little jealousy, as Bartholomew smiled back at Leigh. So far, he'd reserved that expression for Dexter and Leigh. Amanda might not fit in at the True Love, but her son seemed to be a natural.

"Now, dive into those ribs," Leigh said and carried Bartholomew away.

Amanda fought a moment of panic. No one had ever taken her baby away from her before. Her mother wasn't the type to take charge of a squalling infant, and her friends had apparently sensed Amanda's proprietary attitude toward her baby and hadn't reached for him, either. Amanda had been just as glad. Deep down, she believed that if she allowed Bartholomew out of her sight, something terrible would happen to him. It wasn't a rational belief, and she'd have to conquer it if she expected to continue her career, but she wasn't always rational when it came to her son.

Leaving her plate untouched, she craned her neck to see what Leigh was doing with the baby. Showing him off, apparently. Leigh circled the large table of wedding guests, presenting Bartholomew to them all as if he were an heir to the throne. Bartholomew seemed to love it.

"I take it he doesn't get out much."

Startled, she looked up into Chase's green eyes, and her heart began to race. "He's only two months old, after all," she said. "Time enough for him to become a party animal."

"He already has it down. Look at him waving his arms around."

Amanda glanced in Leigh's direction and laughed. "You're right. He seems to love the attention. See how he tried to grab that napkin?"

"He almost got it, too. The kid's got fast hands."

"Maybe he'll grow up to be a magician." Amanda realized they sounded like fond parents at a family gathering. It gave her a disturbingly nice feeling.

Chase turned his back on the scene. "Your dinner's getting cold. And Belinda makes a mighty fine barbecue sauce. Some say Eb Whitlock's is better, but I vote for Belinda's."

"How about you?" She looked up at him. "Have you eaten?"

"Is that an invitation to sit down?"

"Um, sure."

Chase tipped his hat. "Thank you, ma'am." Then he pulled out the chair next to her where Leigh had recently sat and levered his lanky frame into it. "Did you get some rest?"

"Yes, I did." Amanda picked up her knife and fork and began separating the ribs before she attempted to carve off a piece of meat.

"I hope you're going to use your fingers on those. This isn't the Plaza, you know."

Amanda surveyed her plate and regarded her white silk blouse with grave doubt.

"Here's how you handle that problem." Chase took a napkin from the other side of the table, snapped it open and tucked it deftly into the vee of her blouse.

The brush of his fingers against her cleavage lasted a fraction of a second, but it was enough for her to remember that was exactly how he'd begun touching her that fateful night. He'd taken her hand and led her back to the bed built in behind the seats. Then he'd kissed her, taking his time. After all, there was no rush. Almost lazily he'd brushed his knuckles against the vee of her blouse, a blouse like this one, before he'd slipped the first button from its hole ...

Shaken, she gazed at him.

His eyes reflected the flame blazing in hers. "God, Amanda," he murmured.

6

HER HEART RACING, Amanda averted her gaze.

Chase's voice was gentle. "You can't wipe out what happened between us, can you?"

She shook her head.

"If it's any comfort to you, neither can I," he said. "Now, eat your dinner before it gets cold."

She did, because it was the only way she could demonstrate that she'd gained a measure of control. And she used her fingers.

Chase's plate arrived, and he tucked his napkin into the neck of his shirt, gave her a wry smile and began his own meal. A couple of times she sneaked a look at him, and he seemed to be enjoying the food. He polished off a rib and licked his fingers. She remembered all too well how that agile tongue had felt when he'd . . .

She couldn't think about that. "This is very good," she said in an almost-normal tone.

"Told you so."

"Did you have any luck calling today?"

His jaw tightened just a little. "Didn't have time. Leigh needed me to—ah—do some work down at the corrals. By the way, she also said she loaned you some boots. Want to take a ride tomorrow?"

"I could be leaving tomorrow if your phone calls go well tonight."

"Maybe, but if not, you should see some of the country."

The invitation beckoned, and she fought the sinful temptation to spend the day alone with Chase. "I can't go. Don't forget about Bartholomew."

"That's not likely." He pulled his napkin from his shirt and wiped his hands. "But I'll bet we have something around here we could use to carry him in."

"No. It's too dangerous."

"I doubt it." Chase leaned back in his chair. "Besides, don't you need some tourist-type stories to tell your friends back in New York? Otherwise they'll wonder what you spent your time doing out here. You said you wanted to see the saguaros."

"I saw a bunch of them on the way here today."

"Looking out the window of a van is no way to appreciate the desert." He paused. "But then, maybe you don't know how to ride."

"I can ride." She'd once had her own horse, a gorgeous Thoroughbred named Sultan. Her parents still had the ribbons and trophies she and Sultan had won. "I just don't think it's safe to take Bartholomew on a—"

"Let me check into it." He tossed his napkin on the table and pushed his chair back. "I saw Leigh heading into the kitchen. She and Belinda might have an idea how we could transport him. And by the way, when you're ready, I'll walk you back over to the cottage."

"That's not necessary."

He hesitated. "Snakes come out at twilight, Amanda." She stared at him and shuddered.

"I'm sorry if that scares you. But the more you understand the dangers, the safer you'll be, just like in the city. And personally, I'd rather watch out for these kind of snakes than the two-legged ones that live in New York."

She tossed her head. "I'm not afraid in New York."

"You should be." He stood, a flash of anger in his eyes. "The next guy who hauls you out of a snowbank might not have the good manners to ask before he pulls your clothes off."

CHASE WALKED toward the kitchen where he'd seen Leigh and Bartholomew go through the door a moment ago. He wasn't often so short-tempered, but it had been a long time since he'd felt this level of frustration, this much lack of control over his destiny.

Late in the afternoon, he'd learned from Ry that the horse troughs had been contaminated with crushed blister beetles, a substance that could have killed some of the horses if they'd taken in enough of it. Apparently, none of them had, and Freddy had only dosed a few for stomach upset. Ry believed the poisoning was sabotage, but he didn't want to call in the police and risk adverse publicity for the True Love. Chase felt helpless to combat the sabotage if it existed, helpless to protect his investment.

On top of that, Amanda seemed hell-bent on leaving once he gave her the precious information. He'd suggested the ride as a delaying tactic, and it might buy him another day. After that, he was out of ideas to keep her in Arizona. Life had been a damn sight less complicated when he was on the road. Of course, it had been a little lonely, but at least he'd been in control.

Through the steam and bustle of the kitchen he saw Leigh and Belinda standing in a corner seemingly oblivious to the hubbub around them as they cooed at Bartholomew. Chase dodged a waiter carrying a trayful of dirty dishes and eased around one of the cooks spooning barbecue sauce into a plastic storage container. Finally, he made it over to the two women.

"Anybody would think you'd never seen a baby before," he said, putting an arm around Leigh's shoulders.

"That's almost true," Leigh said as she rocked Bartholomew. "Belinda was just saying we don't allow the guests to bring babies, and my wrangling duties don't attract infants, either. So when would I ever be around them?"

"Well, you'd better not get too attached to this one."

Leigh dropped a kiss on Bartholomew's forehead. "It's too late. He won my heart the moment I laid eyes on that dimpled smile."

"He smiles just like his daddy," Belinda said. "Isn't that right, Bartholomew?"

"Stop it, both of you," Chase said. "He's leaving in a couple of days, so just cool it."

Leigh caught him in the pull of her all-knowing eyes. "I'm surprised at you, Chase Lavette. You never struck me as a quitter."

"What do you mean by that crack?"

"You don't want this baby to leave any more than we do. Are you going to let Amanda run off with him without a fight?"

Chase knew there was no point in pretending to Leigh that he didn't want to keep the baby around. She'd been able to read him from the first day they'd spent together. "If you mean take her to court and demand my rights, no, I'm not going to do that."

Belinda stroked the baby's cheek. "I don't know why not. What makes her think she can keep this little bundle all to herself?"

Chase sighed. "Think it through. Amanda's job is in New York. All my money's tied up in this ranch. Let's say I won visitation rights. I'd have to move back to New York, get some minimum-wage job and just hang around. And, on top of it all, I know absolutely nothing about babies. Put me in charge of this kid for a couple of hours and it's panic city."

"Then it's time you got your feet wet." Leigh plopped Bartholomew in his arms. "I have to get ready for a date soon, anyway. And stop limiting your thinking, Chase. There are usually more than two answers to any question, you know."

Leigh's comments barely registered as Chase struggled to adjust his arms around this tiny, squirming human being that was his son. He tried to get his elbow under the baby's head, but Bartholomew kept flopping around. "He's gonna fall," Chase said, his voice rising as Leigh and Belinda giggled. "You women stop your cackling. Leigh, take him back. I don't know how. He's gonna—"

"Easy." Leigh helped him reposition the baby. "Just get your right arm under him and cup his head in that big hand of yours. Good. Then wrap your left around him on the outside. See?"

"I don't know." But Chase did know. As his arms found the new position and the baby quieted, Chase met Bartholomew's rapt gaze. The shock of recognition zinged down to his toes. His son. His flesh and blood. His grip tightened and a lump lodged in his throat.

"Don't let her rob you of this baby," Leigh murmured.

He couldn't speak for fear his voice would crack and give him away. Bartholomew looked like him, for sure, but there was something about the baby's deep stare that stirred a long-dormant memory. His mother, leaning over him . . . just before she walked away.

Bartholomew picked that moment to scrunch up his face and let out a long wail.

"Oh, God." Chase swallowed the lump in his throat and thrust the baby back toward Leigh and Belinda. "I hurt him. I squeezed him too tight. Take him, one of you."

"Stuff and nonsense," Belinda said. "He might be hungry, or need a change, but you didn't hurt him. Babies are tougher than you think. Just carry him back to Amanda."

"Like this? Screaming?"

"I'm sure she's heard it before," Leigh said.

"Yeah, but she's never let me hold him. So the first time she sees me with him, he's crying. What's she going to think of that?"

Leigh smiled. "She might think you're man enough to hold a squalling baby without getting flustered."

"Well, I'm not. I'd rather drive a runaway diesel."

Leigh nudged him toward the kitchen door. "Work on it."

Chase was nearly to the door when he remembered his reason for coming into the kitchen in the first place. He swung around. "Do we have anything around the ranch I could use to carry him on my back? In case Amanda and I take a ride tomorrow," he added when both women looked confused.

Leigh's eyebrows arched. "Now you're talking, cowboy. But I don't know what we might—"

"I do," Belinda said. "Back when you and Freddy were babies, your daddy made a cradleboard, just like the ones the Indians used to carry their little ones. I'm sure it's around here somewhere."

"I haven't a clue what a cradleboard is," Chase said. He'd begun jiggling Bartholomew, and the squalls eased up. Maybe he had to find the right touch, like working with a sensitive clutch.

"It'll work fine," Belinda said. "Just set up your ride."

"Take her up to the pond," Leigh suggested.

"Now, don't you two start getting ideas." Chase swayed gently, soothing the baby even more. "I just thought she should see some of the country as long as she's out here."

Leigh's eyes widened innocently. "Why, I certainly agree, Chase. And I promise not to take any of the dudes on trail rides in that direction tomorrow, so you won't be disturbed while you're showing her the country."

Chase shook his head and started out the kitchen door. Then he turned back again. "You said you have a date tonight? Who with?"

"Edgar."

"The barber? That guy has the personality of a socket wrench, Leigh."

"I know, but I haven't seen a movie in months and it's obvious you won't take me any time soon."

"Somebody needs to improve the quality of your social life."

Leigh waved a hand dismissively. "Feel free to take on my problems after you straighten out your own."

Chase rolled his eyes and turned to leave.

"Nice job with the baby," Leigh called. Her throaty chuckle and Belinda's musical laugh followed him as he used his shoulder to edge out the swinging door into the dining room.

The wedding guests had left, along with Ry and Freddy. Amanda, sitting with her back to the kitchen door, was the only guest still in the room. The clatter of dishes being cleared muffled Chase's approach, allowing him to pause and observe her for a moment. She took a sip of coffee, put the mug down and ran a manicured finger around the edge. He remembered the gesture from the night in the truck.

Despite her jeans and boots, she'd never be mistaken for a cowgirl, he decided. Her hands were the color of milk instead of tanned as a cowgirl's would be, and her jeans were cut too baggy—probably a fashion statement in New York but not in Arizona. He'd become accustomed to the tight jeans Freddy and Leigh wore, which were far more revealing and sexy, yet Amanda's loose-fitting clothing made her all the more mysterious and desirable.

He thought again of how she'd raced from the cottage earlier, barefoot and half-clothed, desperate to save her baby. In that moment, he'd known she would protect Bartholomew with her life. That kind of devotion had a powerful effect on Chase, maybe because he'd never experienced it. But although he admired her protective instincts, they made her vulnerable and in need of protection herself. And that's where, in a perfect world, he would come in. But this wasn't a perfect world.

With a muted sigh, he approached her table.

She turned in her chair, her eyes widening as she noticed he held Bartholomew.

"Leigh . . . told me to bring him to you."

Her gaze softened and he held his breath, wishing he could find a way to keep that tender expression on her face. When she looked like that, hope replaced confusion in his heart. She stood and held out her arms. He'd give a lot to have her do that when he wasn't holding a baby.

"I'd better take him back to the cottage."

He settled Bartholomew in her arms, which couldn't be accomplished without a lot of touching, because he was petrified that he'd let go before Amanda had a firm grip.

Amanda's warm breath caressed his cheek. "I've got him," she murmured.

"Right." He stepped back reluctantly, already missing the weight of his son cradled against his chest.

"Apparently you've held babies before," she said, adjusting Bartholomew's T-shirt over his round tummy.

Chase was immensely pleased. "Some."

"I thought I heard him crying in the kitchen, but you seem to have calmed him down."

"He's probably hungry or needs a change."

"Probably." Amusement lit her eyes. "You sound like the voice of experience. Did you have little brothers and sisters?"

"Uh, no." He glanced away as sudden anger at his mother overtook him. He thought he'd forgiven her for dumping him into the world with no safety net, but apparently he hadn't. "Ready to go?"

"In a minute. Let me put him in his seat."

"Oh, yeah." He watched her position Bartholomew in the plastic carrier. "Belinda says she has something called a cradleboard that I could strap on my back if we want to take that ride tomorrow."

"Is it safe?"

"Freddy and Leigh's father made it for them when they were kids, so I guess it is. The Indians used to carry babies that way."

Amanda lifted the carrier in her arms. "Bartholomew's no papoose."

"He'll be okay. Babies are tougher than you think."

She narrowed her eyes. "If you've never had little brothers or sisters, how come you know so much about babies?"

"I pay attention. Here, let me take him." He relieved her of the infant seat before she had a chance to protest, and felt a rush of pleasure that he had his son back in his grasp. This father business was dangerously habit-forming.

On the way back through the patio he spotted Dexter sitting in his usual corner with Chloe at his feet. "Let's go pick up your bodyguard," he suggested as he walked toward Dexter.

Chloe lifted her head and thumped her tail against the concrete.

"Baby," announced Dexter with a grin.

"Yeah, and its time for him to turn in," Chase said, crouching next to Dexter's chair so the old man could get another look at Bartholomew. "Is it still okay if Chloe stays at the cottage tonight?"

"It's okay." Dexter tucked a bony knuckle under Bartholomew's chin. "Smile, some?"

Bartholomew responded with a gummy grin.

Chase's heart swelled. He could see what Leigh meant about losing her heart to that smile. "He's sure taken a shine to you, Dex."

"Yep."

"Guess we'd better get him tucked in, though."

"Yep." Dexter gave Bartholomew another chuck under the chin before Chase stood, lifting the infant seat.

He grunted as pain squeezed his lower back.

"Chase?" Amanda's forehead puckered with worry.

Great, just what he needed, to wimp out now and show he couldn't even carry his own kid around. "I'm fine," he said.

"It's your back, isn't it? Let me—"

"No, I'm really fine. See you later, Dex."

"Yep."

"And thanks for the loan of Chloe." Chase whistled and the dog came instantly to his side.

"Are you sure you're okay?" Amanda asked as they crossed the patio in the pink light of sunset.

"Yes." The spasm was easing a little, but he desperately needed to get into the pool and swim the laps he'd missed today. Leigh had said stress would make things worse, and as always, she was right.

"Why didn't Dexter eat in the dining room tonight?" Amanda asked.

"He can't take too much confusion. The stroke messed up the circuits in his brain, and he has to concentrate really hard to find the words he wants. He has something called aphasia. When a lot of people are talking, it's an overload situation. Quiet routine is the best thing for him."

Amanda nodded. "And so you just let him stay on, even though he doesn't have a specific function at the ranch. I think that's wonderful. Some efficiency expert would have Dexter out of here in no time."

"But then we'd lose Belinda, and I don't know if the ranch could function without her."

"You mean if something happened to Belinda, Dexter would be out on his ear?"

The idea took Chase by surprise. "No, I guess not. Dexter's as much a part of this ranch as anyone."

"Exactly as I thought. It's nice to see business partners with heart."

Chase fell silent. Affection for the ranch and the people who lived here was sneaking up on him, muddying his thinking. He needed to remember that he still wanted to sell the place one day soon, even if Ry seemed to be waffling on that point these days. Chase had figured out that if he made enough profit on the ranch sale, he might be able to return to New York in style and claim his place as Bartholomew's father. But selling the ranch meant ripping people like Belinda and Dexter out of the only home they'd ever known, as Leigh had so cleverly pointed out today. She knew good and well that would bother his conscience.

They walked along the path, lit by ankle-high landscape lights, the silence punctuated only by the chirp of crickets in the creosote bushes.

"It's beautiful out here this time of day," Amanda said after a while. "I've never seen sunset colors like that, so fiery."

Chase remembered he'd intended to tell her that her hair reminded him of the colors in the evening sky. But that was when he thought they'd be strolling back to the cottage for a night of lovemaking. "It's nice."

"Are you watching for snakes?"

"Sure am. So is Chloe. Guess I could have sent you back with her." He should have thought of that, but of course he'd been determined to protect her himself, while he still had the chance. And he might be about to pay the price. The weight of Bartholomew in the infant seat began to pull at his back muscles. He shifted the burden cautiously.

For the first time in weeks, his back seized up on him. "Damn!"

"What?" She clutched his arm. "A snake?"

"No." He spoke through clenched teeth. "My...back. Take the infant seat." When she'd relieved him of it, he doubled over.

"I'll get help."

"No. Just...give me a minute." He hoped to hell a minute would do it. Chloe nuzzled his hand.

"Can you walk?"

He groaned. "Maybe."

"Then come this way. We're closer to the cottage than we are to the house."

The pain made him too weak to resist as she guided him, hobbling like somebody Dexter's age, up the path. Commanding Chloe to stay with him, she hurried inside the cottage and returned a short time later to help him up the steps and through the door. She closed it behind him.

If he didn't hurt so damned much, he would have laughed. He was inside her cottage at night with the door closed, and he was barely capable of moving, let alone making love. He sank to his hands and knees on the Indian rug, and his hat toppled to the floor in front of him.

Chloe circled him once, obviously unsure whether to help him or guard the baby.

"Go lie down," he rasped. She trotted to one corner and plopped to the floor.

"Tell me what I can do to help," Amanda said just as Bartholomew started to cry.

Chase forced the words out past his pain. "Take care of the baby. And don't step on my hat."

"But you—oh, damn. Okay. I'll change him." She whisked Chase's hat off the floor and out of his sight.

He tried the imaging techniques Leigh had taught him and pictured himself cradled in warmth while gentle fingers worked lovingly at his tortured muscles. The picture wouldn't hold through the steady wailing of his son.

"I guess he's still hungry." Amanda sounded upset. "Let me call someone. Maybe Leigh could—"

"Feed him," Chase muttered. "Leigh's gone for the night."

"All right. I'll feed him."

Chase closed his eyes and imagined himself sliding into hot mineral springs. Hell, he might as well imagine someone handing him a cold beer. Might as well picture Amanda, wearing a string bikini, sliding into the mineral springs with him.

"I have one hand free."

He glanced sideways to see her kneeling on the rug, the nursing baby balanced in the crook of her left arm.

"I can massage with one hand," she said almost impatiently, as if talking to someone who wasn't very bright. "Just tell me how Leigh does it."

Not with her blouse open and a baby at her breast, he thought. But her concern for him had apparently overridden her modesty. And maybe she could ease the bunching of his muscles. "Okay." He took a shallow breath. "The heel of your hand, circular motion, above my belt."

He hadn't expected her to pull his shirttail out to do it, but that was her first move. He found himself dealing with the sweet pressure of her soft hand on his bare skin, and he wanted to weep with frustration. He'd spent hours recalling the intimate nature of her caresses. He'd loved imagining those caresses being repeated, expanded....

"Here?"

"Yes. Harder."

She bore down, and he gasped.

"Too much?"

"No. Keep going." He lowered his head and tried to help with deepening breaths and a conscious loosening of his muscles. Close to his ear the sound of soft sucking reminded him of the nursing baby and unfastened buttons, velvet breasts and firm nipples. As Amanda rose higher on her knees to reach across to his right side, the silk of her blouse brushed against his bare back. Despite his pain, his mouth moistened with need. Then there was the scent of her—that expensive cologne mixed with baby powder and the tantalizing fragrance of mother's milk. He wondered if he'd go insane right here in this little cottage.

"Is it getting any better?"

"Some." Or maybe the intensity of his desire was making him forget the spasm in his back.

"Good. Let me switch Bartholomew."

His peripheral vision had always been excellent, which had been a plus when he'd driven trucks. Now that talent taunted him with a pretty good view of Amanda sitting back on her heels, undoing the other cup of her nursing bra, and giving her right breast to Bartholomew. She didn't bother to fasten the left side.

Maybe she thought he was blind with pain, but if so, she was very mistaken. He took in every detail of each creamy mound, traced with delicate blue veins and crowned with moist tips darkened to burgundy. He'd never realized that a mother nursing her child could be such a turn-on. Sore back or not, he had to get out of here before he humiliated himself by begging.

Clenching his jaw, he brought one booted foot under him.

"What are you doing?"

"Leaving." Sweat stood out on his forehead as he got to his feet. He couldn't stand straight, but he could stand.

"You're in no condition to walk. Let me—"

"You've been a big help," he said, staggering toward the door. "I'll be fine."

"You won't! Let me work on those muscles some more."

He paused, his back to her. "And then what?"

There was a significant silence. "What do you mean?"

"After you've finished the massage, will you refasten your blouse and send me on my way?"

Another silence lengthened between them. "Chase, I was only trying to take care of you. I wasn't trying to seduce you."

"Then I guess the seduction was a bonus. Congratulations." Standing as tall as possible, he hobbled out the door.

7

IT WAS THE WORST NIGHT of Chase's adult life. The only good news was that Ry and Freddy had organized the wedding guests for a boisterous game of Trivial Pursuit and he had the patio to himself. He soaked in the Jacuzzi until his toes wrinkled and then forced himself to swim ten laps. He repeated that routine until he was loose enough to sit through a few telephone calls, but the hour he spent on the phone in his room yielded no answers to Amanda's questions. Finally, he went into the kitchen, pulled a six-pack of beer from the walk-in refrigerator and headed back for some more soaking and laps. Ry came out once to ask if he wanted to join the group and he begged off in the name of pursuing his therapy.

Eventually, the game broke up and everyone trailed off to bed. Chase was sitting in the Jacuzzi, working on his fourth beer and feeling extremely sorry for himself when Leigh arrived home and strolled out to the patio.

She glanced at the beer.

"Help yourself," he said.

"Sure you can spare it? Looks like you need all six."

"Be nice to me, Leigh."

She unhooked a can of beer from a plastic ring and popped the top. "Your back went out tonight, didn't it?"

"Among other things. How was your date?"

"Boring." She pulled up a chaise longue and sat on the edge of it. "We didn't laugh at the same jokes in the movie."

"Bad sign."

"Yeah." She stood up and patted the chaise. "Come on up here and let me work the kinks out for you."

"You don't have to."

"Don't be an idiot, Lavette. That macho pride doesn't cut any ice with me."

"Okay, okay." He climbed out gingerly, using the steps and the rail. Yesterday he would have been able to hoist himself out using his arms. "I hate this."

"I suspect you were a little too proud of your male physique, my friend. The universe has a way of evening things out."

"The universe has been chopping away at me ever since the day I was born." Chase eased himself face-down on the chaise. "I'm so far from even, it's pathetic."

"My, we are into self-pity tonight."

Chase muttered an oath.

"Well, pain does put people in a foul mood," Leigh said, sounding more sympathetic. She dropped to her knees and began an expert massage of his back.

At her touch, Chase could feel the healing begin. "You have a real gift for this, Leigh. You could set up a clinic and charge people." He congratulated himself on coming up with the perfect solution to what Leigh would do once the ranch sold. He'd been thinking about that tonight, as if he didn't have enough to worry about.

"Nope." Leigh leaned into the massage. "I have a theory that once I started charging, I'd lose my abilities. Did you know I'm also a water witch?"

"A what?"

"I can find water with a forked stick. I've been able to do it ever since I was a little girl. But my dad warned me never to charge for the service, or I'd lose the gift. I think it's the same with massage."

Chase sighed. Another of his great plans down the drain. But his back was improving radically. He considered it one of the great mysteries of nature that Leigh could give him a rubdown and he felt no sexual arousal at all. One soft caress from Amanda, however, and he was a basket case.

Leigh paused to sip her beer. "Did Belinda find that cradleboard?"

"I don't know, but it doesn't matter. I wouldn't dare take Amanda and the baby out."

"Why not?"

"Look at me! What if my back seized up out on the trail?"

"I guess you could ride home facedown over the saddle."

"Not funny, Leigh." *Ride home.* How easily she'd said that. Home wasn't a foreign concept to Leigh, but it was to Chase, who'd never allowed himself to call anyplace home. When an apartment got too cozy, he moved, just to keep in practice. He'd become very good at leaving.

"I'd give it a try," she said.

He had to think for a moment to remember what she was talking about. Oh, yeah. The horseback ride with Amanda.

"I gather you don't have much time to settle things between you two," Leigh added.

"That's right."

Leigh resumed the massage. "The way I see it, your best hope is to get her to bring Bartholomew back to the ranch every few months. If she has a good time here, she might be more willing to do that."

"Define a good time."

Leigh chuckled. "Oh, no. I'll leave that up to you. But it's evident your charms worked on her once before."

"Are you telling me to seduce her?"

"I'm telling you to make use of your strong points, cowboy." She gave him a sharp whack on the butt. "Now get back in the pool and do ten more laps. I'm going to bed."

WHEN AMANDA AWOKE the next morning, the first thing she saw was Chase's black Stetson dangling from the bedpost where she'd tossed it the evening before. Bartholomew had gotten her up once during the night to nurse, and now he and Chloe were sound asleep. As the room filled with pink light, Amanda snuggled under the covers and contemplated Chase's hat. The black felt bore scuff marks on the crown, as if it had landed in the dirt a few times, and the brim dipped down in front, as if molded that way when Chase had repeatedly tugged it low over his eyes.

She remembered her first glimpse of him in the hat when she'd stepped from the jetway. On a virile man like Chase, a black Stetson was almost overkill. Now that she thought about it, she could trace her loss of detachment from her first encounter with his hat.

Then he'd compounded the hero effect by charging in after the snake, and after that, by holding her while she'd cried. But maybe she could have dismissed those incidents, even turned her back on the desires he'd stirred in her, if only he hadn't walked toward her, still wearing that darned hat, and carrying Bartholomew. She hadn't anticipated how she'd feel seeing their son in his arms.

Had Chase and Bartholomew been strangers, it still would have been a compelling picture—a rugged cowboy whose big, work-roughened hands cradled a tender little baby. But they were not strangers. Chase was the man who had made such beautiful love to her months ago, and Bartholomew was the stunning result. The image of Chase holding their child would haunt her for the rest of her life.

On the bedside table the telephone buzzed. She reached for it quickly.

"Good morning, Amanda."

She closed her eyes at the sound of his voice and curled the cloth-covered telephone cord around her finger. "Good morning, Chase."

"I know it's early, but we ought to beat the heat if we're going up into Rogue Canyon today."

"Are we? What about your back?"

"My back's fine. Belinda found the cradleboard and she's packing us a lunch. I'll have Duane bring the horses up to the house so we don't have to fool with driving down to the corrals. How soon can you be ready?"

"I, ah, imagine because of your back you didn't have a chance to make any calls last night."

"Actually, I did. I thought we could talk about it up in the canyon. It's a beautiful spot, Amanda."

She hesitated, then succumbed. "Give me twenty minutes."

"Great."

"Unless Bartholomew's poky about eating. Then I might need longer."

"I'll be waiting in the dining room with a cup of coffee for you."

"That would be nice." She played with the telephone cord, pretending she was in an old black-and-white movie. "I take sugar."

"I know." He sounded as if he might be smiling. "Tons of sugar."

Then she remembered the cups of coffee they'd shared in the cab of his truck and how he'd teased her about the amount of sugar she put in hers. And later, when he'd sampled nearly every inch of her body, he'd said, "I know why you taste so sweet. It's all that sugar you put in your coffee."

"Amanda? Are you still there?"

She took a shaky breath. "Yes, I'm still here." She glanced up at the bedpost. "I have your hat."

"Wear it. I have another one. See you soon." Then he was gone.

Amanda held the phone to her ear a moment longer as she gazed at the hat. He loved that hat. Even in the midst of his agony the night before, he'd warned her not to step on it. Her heart beat faster. Perhaps she was being wooed.

Probably because she was impatient to get out the door, Bartholomew seemed to nurse more slowly and wouldn't burp for her. Accustomed to meeting deadlines and arriving on time for appointments, she was irritated at being five minutes later than she'd estimated when she dashed out the door with Chloe trotting by her side. She'd thrown a clean diaper over her shoulder to protect her blouse in case Bartholomew decided to burp or worse on the way to the main house.

Instead of braiding her hair as she'd intended, she'd settled for the quicker solution of tying it back with a silk scarf. Chase's hat was slightly big, but she loved the way it looked when she pulled it down in front, the way Chase wore it. And the brim offered wonderful protection from the sun, which already felt warm on her shoulders.

When she opened the patio gate and stepped inside, she was greeted with bedlam as Belinda supervised the stringing of thousands of tiny white lights, the placement of tables and chairs and the arrangement of baskets of huge paper flowers from Mexico. Some of the guests were attempting to help, while others had abandoned the idea in favor of a swim, which caused more commotion as they were warned not to splash and damage any of the decorations.

Dexter sat in a shady alcove watching the proceedings. Chloe's breakfast was in a dish beside him.

"Go on, girl," Amanda said, stroking the dog's head. "And thanks." As Chloe navigated the crowded patio toward her owner, Amanda waved at Dexter. "Thank you," she called. "She made me feel much safer."

Dexter waved back. "Yep!"

Belinda turned, a string of lights in her hand, and smiled at Amanda. "The cradleboard's all ready."

"Are you sure it'll work okay?"

"Absolutely. Freddy and Leigh spent hours in it when they were babies. Now go have fun."

Amanda had noticed how Belinda doted on Bartholomew, and took heart from the woman's confidence in the cradleboard. "I'll do that," she said, returning Belinda's smile.

She skirted a man carrying a ladder and nearly bumped into Leigh and Freddy, who were walking across the patio deep in discussion.

Leigh surveyed Amanda's outfit and nodded in satisfaction. "You're looking more and more like a cowgirl. I guess you're going on that ride."

"I guess I am. And I'm late."

"Don't sweat it," Freddy said. "With Chase still around, Ry had an excuse to hide out in the dining room and drink coffee instead of coming out here to help decorate."

Amanda adjusted Bartholomew against her other shoulder. "Did Chase mention he had a problem with his back last night?"

"Yes," Leigh said. "And as his unofficial nurse, I urged him to go. He's borrowing Ry's cellular telephone, so if you have any trouble you can call the ranch for help."

"Oh!" Amanda hadn't expected such amenities as cellular phones at a place like the True Love. Her anxiety level dipped considerably. "That's a terrific idea."

"The phone works even up in Rogue Canyon," Freddy said. "I didn't want to get one, but Ry insisted and now I love it."

"It makes me feel a lot better about going up there with Bartholomew," Amanda said, "although I hate to leave you with all this work and take Chase away, on top of it."

Freddy waved a hand dismissively. "The work will get done, and you shouldn't go back to New York without a ride up to Rogue Canyon. Besides, it's cooler up there."

"If you're sure . . ."

"We're sure," Freddy said. "Go find Chase. And tell Ry he's needed out here."

"Cancel that last part," Leigh said. "Freddy and I have to get something straight before her beloved groom shows up. Just go, Amanda, and have a great time."

"Thanks." As Amanda started toward the French doors leading into the house, she overheard a few words as Leigh turned to Freddy.

"Before he comes out, promise me you'll tell him you're allergic to roses."

"But then I'll never get roses my whole married life!"

"Maybe he'll go for diamonds, instead."

Amanda decided against trying to puzzle out the meaning of the exchange as she headed for the dining room.

Sure enough, Ry and Chase were in a far corner hunched over coffee mugs, a third one steaming by Chase's elbow right next to the cellular phone. A disreputable-looking brown hat pulled down over Chase's forehead made him look more like a rogue than a gentleman, but his idea of using the cellular phone showed that he was obviously taking his responsibility for her and Bartholomew seriously. A rogue who took his responsibilities seriously. It was a tantalizing combination.

Both Chase and Ry glanced up and started to rise as she approached.

"Please don't get up," she said, touched by the courtly gesture.

Ry sank back to his seat but Chase moved toward her.

"Let me hold him so you can drink your coffee." He'd extricated Bartholomew from her arms before she could protest.

"You'd better take this diaper to protect your shirt." She tried to hand it to him but he shook his head. "Chase, you—"

"I'll be fine." His eyes had a stubborn gleam.

"If you say so." She sat down in the chair he'd just vacated. "Good luck."

"I don't need special equipment just to hold you, do I, son?" Chase hoisted Bartholomew to his shoulder with a manly heave.

Bartholomew responded by upchucking down the back of Chase's shirt.

Chase's eyes widened but he kept his grip on the baby. "Damn. I think his radiator just overflowed."

Amanda tried not to laugh, but Ry was chuckling gleefully, and finally she couldn't help herself. "I warned you. You'd better put that shirt in to soak and get a clean one." She held out her arms. "I'll take him so you can go do that."

"No, *I'll* take the little buckaroo," Ry said. "But I'm not too manly to wear a diaper over my shoulder while I do it. Give him to me, Chase. I might as well get in shape. I have a feeling Freddy's going to be in the market for a couple of these pretty soon."

"Hold him real careful," Chase said, relinquishing control of the baby with obvious reluctance. "Get both hands under him. Support his head. Not like that, like this." He adjusted the baby in Ry's arms.

Amanda brought her coffee mug to her lips to hide her smile.

Ry frowned as Chase kept repositioning his grip. "Hell, Chase, I think I can hold a baby without you giving me lessons."

"Don't cuss in front of him, either."

"Why not? You did when he barfed on you."

"He caught me by surprise. No, move your arm a little the other way. He likes it better if you—"

"Will you *leave*?" Ry glared at Chase. "I never knew you were such a fussbudget, Lavette."

"I'm leaving." Chase backed away and adjusted his hat. "Don't drop him."

"Oh, for crying out loud."

After Chase left, Ry shook his head. "The boy's gone haywire. By the way, do you want anything to eat? The kitchen's a disaster, but I'm sure we can round up a cinnamon roll or something."

"Coffee's fine." She took another drink of the warm liquid, which was the perfect temperature and sweetened exactly as she liked it.

"I envy you two riding out of here today," Ry said. "If I didn't think Freddy would have my head on a pole, I'd go with you."

"She did mention something about your hiding out in here so you wouldn't have to help," Amanda said.

Ry grinned, and Amanda glimpsed the good humor that Freddy must have fallen in love with. "I don't stand a chance," Ry said. "That woman's had my number since day one."

"It looks like an pretty even contest to me."

Ry gazed at her, his smile softening. "All I know is, she's the one. I'm a lucky man to be marrying Freddy Singleton tomorrow."

An unexpected lump formed in Amanda's throat at the tender admission. "I wish you both the best."

"Just keep your fingers crossed that the horses don't buck. I should have my head examined for agreeing to this wedding on horseback. At least you'll have something unique to tell your friends in New York."

"I . . . may not be here for the wedding."

"Oh? I thought your reservation here ran through the week."

She glanced away from him. "It does, but I think it would be best for all concerned if I left sooner. Chase said he had some information for me on his family's medical history. He thought I should see the canyon before I go, and he'll give me the information while we ride, I guess. I'll probably catch a night flight out."

"Have you made plane reservations?"

"No." She looked at him and her chest tightened. "Perhaps I should do that now."

His gaze was speculative. "No rush. Flights usually aren't crowded this time of year."

The tightness in her chest eased. "I suppose not. And I don't know exactly when we'll be back from the ride."

"Or how it'll go."

She swallowed. "That's not really—"

"For the record, I think Chase deserves a chance to be a father to this baby."

She gasped at his directness. The charming good humor was gone from his expression and she remembered he was also a high-powered commodities broker. In retaliation, she adopted her big-city, don't-mess-with-me attitude. "I don't believe that it's any of your business."

"He's my partner." Ry's blue eyes narrowed. "That makes it my business. I've advised him to take you to court if necessary, and I'm in contact with lawyers who could win the case, hands down, but he won't discuss that option, so I'm appealing to you. Do the right thing, Amanda."

"I believe I am doing the right thing!"

"Then I guess we have a difference of opinion on the matter." Ry stood and walked around the table. "If you'll excuse me, I think I'll go out and help Freddy with the decorations." He handed Bartholomew to her with care, but there was no smile on his face. "Chase would have wanted a connection with his son even if he'd never seen him, but now that you've brought the baby out here, you can't just snatch him away. If Chase is the man I think he is, he won't allow it. Have a nice ride." Then he tipped his hat and left the room.

Bartholomew began to fuss and Amanda rocked him against her as she tried to regain her composure. It was difficult. Everything Ry had said had struck a nerve and challenged her sense of fair play. And he was right that she'd have the same moral dilemma whether she'd come to Arizona or not. The trip had simply brought it to a head sooner.

"Where's Ry?" Chase asked, striding into the room.

"He, um, decided to go out and help with the decorations."

"You're kidding." Chase glanced in the direction of the patio. "He told me he'd rather shovel a corral of manure than arrange paper flowers in a basket." He shrugged. "Oh, well. Ready to go?"

She could tell him she'd changed her mind and insist that they talk about the medical history now. Then she could book a flight out this morning and leave the True Love and all the conflict it caused within her. Except she knew her problems couldn't be solved that simply anymore.

8

A HALF HOUR LATER, Amanda had plenty of time to contemplate the wonders of a cradleboard as she rode on a gray mare named Pussywillow. Ahead of her, Chase, mounted on a bay gelding named Mikey, carried Bartholomew on his back. Chase had assured her that Mikey was the steadiest horse the True Love owned.

Amanda had been introduced to Rosa, the head housekeeper, who'd shown them how to wrap Bartholomew securely in a blanket and lace him inside the cradleboard, which was made of leather, not wood as she'd imagined. He looked like a little mummy with only his face peeping out. Even that was protected from the sun with a leather hood projecting from the top of the board. Apparently, the arrangement suited Bartholomew. After a huge yawn, he fell asleep.

A western saddle felt cumbersome to Amanda after riding English all her life, but she loved having a horse under her again. Pussywillow had a soft mouth and responded to Amanda's slightest pressure on the bit. Amanda knew instinctively the little mare would be terrific at a fast lope, and she battled her impatience at the slow pace of the ride.

But slow was the only way to take Bartholomew along, so she settled back and savored the rolling gait of her horse and a luxurious sense of freedom. It had been months, ten to be exact, since she'd been on an outing with an attractive man. Raising her son alone had seemed like a liberating thing to do until she'd actually had the baby and realized how drastically her life had become circumscribed by her new role. She had no idea how she'd successfully resume a career that required the same single-minded dedication her son demanded.

This morning, however, with Chase carrying Bartholomew, she felt unencumbered, a little less like an overburdened mother and a lot more like a woman—a desirable woman. The pleasant friction of the saddle against her thighs and the constant view of Chase's broad shoulders and narrow hips drew her thoughts once again to that night in the truck cab.

She and Chase seemed destined to meet during temperature extremes. That night she'd been in danger of freezing to death. Today perspiration trickled between her breasts. She unfastened her canteen, unscrewed the lid and took a drink. Then she dabbed some water on her neck and between her breasts. A swim in the pond would be nice, but of course she'd brought no bathing suit. . . .

Wanting to hear the sound of Chase's voice, she cast around for a neutral topic of conversation. "Does it ever rain here?" she finally asked.

"They tell me it does," he replied over his shoulder. "But I've never seen it. Sometime after the Fourth of July it's supposed to rain nearly every afternoon, and that goes on until September, but here we are in the middle of July and not a drop. The desert's dry as a tinderbox. Leigh keeps threatening to stage a rain dance."

"After the wedding."

Chase laughed. "Yeah. After the wedding."

She liked his laugh. She hadn't heard it all that much since she'd arrived.

He guided his horse into a clearing dominated by a pile of clay-colored rubble. "And speaking of the wedding, this is where it will take place at nine in the morning. Almost twenty-four hours from now, as a matter of fact."

"Here?" It seemed a most unremarkable spot to her.

"It's the original homestead of Thaddeus and Clara Singleton. Leigh told me it was built in 1882 and the walls were still standing until a couple of months ago. A stampede flattened the house the day I got here."

"Belinda told me about the stampede. And the smashed lintel with the True Love brand on it. Aren't they mounting it on an easel or something for the ceremony?"

"Yeah." Chase adjusted the cradleboard straps over his shoulders.

"Is your back okay?"

"So far, so good." He surveyed the clearing. "You know, it doesn't seem like much of a place for a wedding. When I was living on the road, I saw the perfect wedding church in Upstate New York, sitting smack-dab in the middle of a green meadow. White clapboard siding, stained-glass windows, a steeple and a bell. I thought about stopping, but I was late for a delivery. Didn't matter, anyway. I never planned on getting married."

Some of her sensual fog slipped away. "I know. You told me that."

He glanced over at her. "I did? When?"

"After we . . . while we were driving home, when we discussed whether we should see each other again. I didn't think it was a good idea, and you said I was probably right, because I looked like the type who might get serious, and you had no intention of letting that happen with any woman."

He studied her for several moments. "Is that one of the reasons you didn't tell me about the baby?"

"Yes."

He dropped his gaze and swore softly.

Hope ignited by Ry's statements earlier burst into flame within her. "Did I misunderstand you?"

He raised his head and gave her a long, level look. "No, you didn't," he said at last. He reined his horse around. "We'd better go on. It's getting hot."

Amanda rode along the path lined with bleached-out bushes and bristling cacti and wondered what she was doing on this stupid outing. She usually liked being right, but in this case it hurt like hell. Chase was exactly what he'd proclaimed himself to be in the first place, a drifter who wanted no entanglements. He might expect some contact with his son, on his terms, but he wasn't about to beg her to marry him and establish a traditional home together. And she also had to face an unsettling truth about herself. Increasingly, she wanted him to do exactly that.

Not that she'd come to Arizona with that in mind, at least not consciously, but every moment with Chase had made the idea seem less crazy, especially when she saw him with Bartholomew. Then he'd practically insisted on this ride so they could be alone, and he'd offered her his hat to wear. Silly her, she'd thought he might be moving in the same direction she was. Obviously not.

The trail wound upward as they worked their way into the canyon along a dry creek bed. Granite cliffs rose ever higher on either side of them. There was no sound save the crunching of the horses' hooves in the sand, the creak of leather and the muted drone of insects. Amanda realized she'd never been out of reach of traffic noise. Lured by the absence of civilization's clamor, Amanda began to fantasize what it might have been like for a frontierswoman and her man carving out a life in the desert.

It would have been physically very difficult, but that might have forged a stronger bond. Men and women seemed to depend on each other more back then. Except for the drifters, she thought with a grimace. The frontier had fostered its share of those, too, and Chase Lavette was a throwback if ever she'd seen one. He needed the equivalent of a string of dance-hall girls and no children whatsoever. Ry McGuinnes could think what he wanted, but Chase wasn't the type to be tied down by a wife or a baby.

"The pond's just over there, up where those cotton-woods are," Chase said, pointing.

She sighed in audible relief at the sight of a swath of emerald green tucked into the canyon ahead of them.

He turned slightly in his saddle. "Are you going to make it?"

She straightened, not wanting his concern. "Of course. I rode Thoroughbreds in competition when I was a teenager. It's not the riding. It's the heat. I can't believe Bartholomew's still asleep. I bet he'll be soaked with sweat."

Chase faced forward again. "I guess it wasn't such a good idea, coming up here."

"Then why did you suggest it?"

"God knows, Amanda. But we're almost there, so we might as well spend some time near the pond and cool off a little."

The horses apparently smelled the water and quickened their pace. Within minutes, they'd climbed past the rock-and-earth dam barricading the creek, and Amanda caught her first glimpse of the pond. Huge cotton-woods, their trunks dappled gray and white, grew beside the sandy bank, shading the oasis created by the pond. Amanda had already learned the dramatic differ-

ence between sun and shade. Shade next to water looked
like heaven.

They dismounted and tethered the horses to a low-
hanging branch.

"Let me help you get that cradleboard off," Amanda
said as she crossed to Chase.

"Thanks." He lifted the straps away from his shoulders and Amanda took the weight of baby and carrier.
She noticed the dark stain of sweat covering Chase's back
before she returned her attention to her baby. Bartholomew opened his eyes and blinked.

"Hello. Trip's over, sweetheart." Amanda settled the
board on the sand and unlaced the fastenings.

"Is he okay?"

"Just a little sweaty and hungry," Amanda said without glancing up. The cool shade had improved her mood
a bit. "He'll be fine after I change and feed him."

"Then I think I'll take a swim if you don't need anything right now."

"Oh." She glanced up and saw him already stripping
away his shirt. The pewter medallion winked in the sun.
"That sounds wonderful. Do you swim here often?"

"Whenever the pool in the patio is too crowded to do
my laps."

Sweat trickled down her back and she cast a look of
longing at the pond.

"You can go in after you've fed Bartholomew. I'll watch
him."

"I...didn't bring a suit." She pulled Bartholomew out
of the wrapped blanket and stood, holding his damp little body against her shoulder.

"Neither did I." He sat on a rock and pulled off his
boots. "Didn't think I'd go swimming, but I should have
figured I'd need it after carrying the baby."

"Well, I have no suit and no excuse of a bad back."

He stood and unbuckled his belt. "So what? Swim in your underwear and sit in the sun until it dries." He unbuttoned his jeans and shoved them over his hips. Then he glanced at her. "You're staring, Amanda."

Her face grew hot and she turned toward her horse, where she'd packed extra diapers in the saddlebag. "I'm just not as casual about these things as you are, I guess."

"The hell you're not. At least not around me, for some reason."

She jerked her head up to meet his challenging gaze. "If you're referring to last night—"

"Yes, I'm referring to last night. I've been thinking about that, and I've decided you knew, on some level, how you were affecting me, breastfeeding while you gave me a back massage. You were flirting with me, Amanda."

"I was not! It was an emergency and I couldn't come up with any other solution." But a guilty conscience pricked her. Perhaps she had enjoyed teasing him, just a bit, under the guise of ministering to him. Maybe she'd enjoyed it a lot. And she was furious with him for figuring it out.

"Well, this is an emergency and I can't come up with any other solution." Chase kicked away his jeans and walked toward the pond. She drew in a quick breath. The last time she'd seen him, his body had been white as sculpted marble, but weeks of swimming and sunning at this pool had transformed him into a bronzed god. He strode into the water, flexed his back muscles and executed a shallow dive. He was, she concluded, definitely flirting with her. And the effect was exactly what he would have wished.

While Chase swam, Amanda changed Bartholomew and found a large cottonwood tree to sit against. From her position slightly above the pond, she watched Chase's steady, clean strokes through the water while she nursed the baby. The pond was bigger than she'd expected, at least fifty or sixty yards at its longest point. Chase swam to within a few feet of the shore, where he turned and started back across. Patches of sunlight gilded his shoulders, and the reeds bordering the far edge of the pond swayed in the current he created.

His graceful movement seduced her with memories of the fluid surge of his hips as he'd loved her. That night in the truck nothing had seemed important but the melding of two bodies. Now that she had time to reflect, what amazed her was the effortless way they'd come together, how synchronized their rhythm had been from the start.

That rhythm seemed to have followed them to this glade. It echoed in his purposeful stroke through the water, the pulsing buzz of insects, the suckling of their child at her breast. The air smelled warm and ripe, and she vibrated to the subliminal beat, unable to stop herself from slipping into the sensuous cadence.

When he left the water, she wasn't surprised when he walked toward her with deliberate strides, as if in time to the unheard rhythm. He dropped to one knee beside her, his gaze on the nursing baby. He reached out to stroke the downy head, and she sighed.

"Amanda. I don't want to fight with you."

She lifted her head slowly. "Then let's not fight."

His hand still cupping the baby's head, he looked at her, his eyes as green as the sunlit canopy of trees. Slowly, he reached behind her and gently untied the scarf from her hair. It floated to the ground as he used his fingers to comb her hair forward until it shimmered in a fiery curtain just above where Bartholomew clung to her breast.

His eyes grew shadowy with desire as he gazed at her, and her breathing quickened.

Carefully, he leaned toward her. Her eyelids drifted closed in surrender when his lips, cool from the pond, touched hers with no more pressure than a falling leaf fluttering to the ground. She met his gentleness with her own, warming his mouth as if in apology for all the hurt they'd showered on each other. She leaned into the kiss, balancing herself with one hand against the powerful bulge of his biceps. It flexed beneath her touch, coolness turning to heat. Then, before the heat could turn to fire, he pulled away.

She opened her eyes again. His gaze probed hers. "You were right," she whispered, her lips tingling, wanting more. "I am afraid of you."

He brushed her cheek with his knuckles. "I don't want to make problems." His voice was husky. "But I can't let you walk out of my life and never come back."

She thought of what Ry had said. "Because... because of Bartholomew?"

He hesitated. "No, not just because of Bartholomew."

"But a little while ago you just said you don't want entanglements." Her heart hammered as she gazed into his eyes.

He slid his hand behind her neck and massaged gently. "Yeah, and I'll probably say it again at some stupid moment. For years I've guarded my freedom like a junkyard dog. Old habits die hard."

"Sometimes they never die."

"Just bear with me a while, Amanda."

With a shuddering sigh, Bartholomew drew their attention down to where he clung to Amanda's breast.

"I love watching you nurse him." Chase outlined the curve of the baby's cheek with one finger. "That's another thing I shouldn't have said. Maybe you were flirting with me last night. Maybe you were just acting natural. Whichever it was, I'd never want you to be embarrassed about doing this in front of me."

"For some reason, I haven't been," she murmured. "Not even that first time in the van."

"Good." He traced a path along Bartholomew's chin and continued the caress over the fullness of Amanda's breast.

She gasped and looked up at him.

His gaze was fathomless as he continued to trace soft patterns over her breast. "I've never wanted a woman the way I want you," he said softly. "I haven't wanted to admit that, for fear I'd jeopardize my precious freedom, but it's true. I know it's not convenient for either of us, but you're driving me crazy." His mouth curved in a smile and his dimple flashed. "From the look in your eyes, I think you feel the same way."

She had trouble breathing. "Chase, we can't—"

"I know." He glanced down at Bartholomew. "But I couldn't resist touching you, just this once." He levered himself away from her with a sigh. "And once is about all I can manage without forgetting myself."

She almost moaned in frustration. He was right, though. They couldn't keep playing with fire when they had a baby to consider. Bartholomew loosened his grip on her nipple and gazed up at her, as if to remind her of that fact. He needed to be changed, and she had to figure out where he could be settled for a short nap. "Where's a safe place for him to sleep?" she asked as she refastened her nursing bra.

"That depression between the exposed tree roots should make a perfect bed for him."

She studied the spot Chase had indicated and decided it would work. "There's another blanket and a clean diaper in my saddlebag, if you wouldn't mind getting them."

"I'll do better than that. I'll change him for you."

"You will?" She looked up and discovered he was already halfway across the clearing.

"Sure," he called over his shoulder. "With those sticky tab things instead of pins it should be a cinch."

Amanda was touched by his eagerness to participate. She'd read once that a new father's willingness to help could be destroyed if the mother hovered around offering suggestions. Difficult as it would be for her, she'd let him change Bartholomew without interference.

Chase returned with the blanket and diaper. He folded the blanket and arranged it in the natural depression between two cottonwood roots, put the fresh diaper to one side, and held out his arms for the baby. She gave him Bartholomew with what she hoped was an encouraging smile.

"Okay, buddy," Chase said, settling the baby on the blanket and pulling at the tabs fastening the old diaper. "Time for an oil and lube job."

Amanda kept quiet as he wrestled with the fastenings. When he leaned closer, his medallion dangled within Bartholomew's reach. Gurgling happily, the baby grabbed it and pulled, nearly throwing Chase off-balance. Amanda pretended not to notice.

The diaper came off in shreds, but Chase finally removed it. "This doesn't seem very wet," he said, glancing at Amanda. "We may have wasted a perfectly good—"

"Chase, look out." But the warning came too late. A steady stream rose in the air as if from the nozzle of a miniature fire hose.

As it splattered against Chase's neck and ran down his chest, he yelped in surprise. "It's a gusher!"

Amanda couldn't hold her laughter another second. "I forgot to warn you," she gasped, holding her sides. "Sometimes when fresh air hits, he—"

"No kidding." His attempt to look stern was marred by the amusement dancing in his green eyes. "At least I know the equipment works."

"I'll finish up if you want to go wash in the pond."

Chase got to his feet with a show of dignity. "Guess I'll take you up on that. Next time I'll be ready."

Next time. Amanda smiled at the pleasant sound of that promise as she diapered Bartholomew while Chase cleaned off in the pond.

Soon he was back. "You can swim now if you want," he said, kneeling next to Bartholomew.

She considered the welcome treat versus the wisdom of undressing in this sensually charged atmosphere. "I don't think that's a good idea."

He glanced up. "If you think I'll be tempted to make love to you if you take off your clothes, you're right. But if you think I'll forget about Bartholomew and seduce you on the spot, you don't know me very well."

She couldn't resist a smile. "That's the whole point. I don't know you very well."

"Then it's time to learn. The water's cool. And you look—if you'll excuse the expression—hot."

And so she was. She wanted to take off her clothes, all right. But not necessarily to go swimming. Considering their obligation to keep a watchful eye on Bartholomew, swimming was the safer option. "All right," she said, turning toward the pond.

She walked down to the narrow strip of sand beside the water and unbuttoned her blouse. She didn't look to see if he was watching, pretty certain that he would be. A large boulder provided a seat while she pulled off her boots and stuffed her socks into them before placing them next to Chase's on the sand. Then she wriggled her bare toes in pleasure. Before she'd come to Arizona, she'd treated herself to a pedicure—the salon hadn't minded that she held Bartholomew on her lap during the procedure—and her toes were tipped in cranberry. Of course, her decision to get a pedicure had nothing to do with the fact that Chase had remarked on her delicate feet the night they'd made love. Of course not. She was beginning to wonder just how much she'd been fooling herself.

As she stood and unfastened the waistband of her jeans, she felt a little like a nightclub stripper performing for a single customer. She was unsettled to discover the idea exciting. She remembered that she'd worn a favorite pair of silk bikinis under her jeans. Cut high, they were trimmed around each leg with a ruffle of Belgian lace. When she stepped out of her jeans, she imagined she heard Chase catch his breath. But it could have been a lizard moving through dry leaves beneath the trees. She'd seen several today, harmless little creatures with no teeth. Still, she walked toward the water as if she were a model on a runway, admitting to herself that she wanted him to want her.

At the edge of the pond, sand gave way to mossy rocks, and her graceful entrance into the water was marred by some hobbling until she finally launched herself with a satisfying splash. Ah. For a moment, she forgot about Chase as she slipped along in a slow crawl, her self-made current swirling past her body and cleansing away the dust and sweat of the ride. She'd only been swimming in private pools and Long Island Sound, and she kept expecting either the taste of chlorine or salt. This water held neither, and she rolled to her back like an otter, reveling in the pond's crystal perfection. No wonder Chase loved swimming here.

She floated for a while, her hair billowing out around her, and gazed up through the leaves to the blue sky beyond. Life at the ranch was the complete opposite of her life in the city. Work there was indoors and cerebral; work at the ranch was outdoors and physical. She'd probably be bored in no time out here. It was okay for a change of pace, but she needed intellectual stimulation, the thrill of business competition, the—

Something yanked at the hem of her panties. After her experience the day before, all she could imagine were water moccasins. She flipped over in a panic and swallowed some water. Another yank, this time from the front. With a yelp, she propelled herself through the water. "Chase!" she burbled, scrambling over the rocks. "Chase!"

He ran to meet her, catching her by the elbows and hauling her up onto the bank.

"Something tried to bite me," she cried, her arms automatically going around him as she shivered. "I think it was a water moccasin."

He enclosed her in arms warmed by sunlight and brought her against his chest. She laid her cheek there. As she listened to the rapid thud of his heart, her gaze rested on the pewter medallion that moved gently with his breathing. He'd put his jeans back on—she felt the brush of denim against her bare legs and wished he hadn't, wished . . . but that wasn't wise. As she slowly stopped shivering, she realized he was shaking with silent laughter.

"I forgot to tell you about the fish," he said, chuckling. He tugged playfully at the Belgian lace decorating her panties. "They were probably after this."

She sagged in his arms. "Fish," she mumbled, feeling stupid. "I can deal with fish."

"There's nothing dangerous in that water." Chase had abandoned the lace and now cupped one hand under her bottom. "I wouldn't have let you go in if there had been."

She stayed very still as he pressed her closer and his heartbeat grew louder. Beneath his jeans he was hard as stone.

"But there is danger right here," he murmured against her wet hair. "Because now that I have you in my arms, I don't want to let you go."

9

HEAT SEARED through Amanda's veins, bringing a flush to her chilled skin. She moaned softly. Then she lifted her head and gazed upward into Chase's passion-filled eyes. "Bartholomew," she whispered in a voice heavy with disappointment.

"Yes, Bartholomew." With a sigh he released her and averted his eyes. "I'll get the sandwiches and canteens if you'll go check on him. When you called from the pond, he was still asleep."

Biting her lower lip in frustration, Amanda picked her way across rocks and sandy ground toward the tree where Bartholomew lay cradled between the exposed roots. He was still fast asleep and looking like an angel with his little snub nose and his tiny mouth pursed as if ready to give her a kiss. Except that Bartholomew's kiss wasn't the one she wanted at the moment. She loved her baby, loved him to distraction. But she hadn't anticipated the vigilance he'd require. Or the sacrifices.

She sat on a large section of root and combed her fingers through her wet hair as Chase came toward her, a canteen slung over one tanned shoulder, a bag of sandwiches in one hand and his shirt in the other.

He handed her the shirt. "I'd appreciate it if you'd put this on. You don't have to button it or anything, just . . . put it on."

She glanced down at her damp underwear and understood his point. When wet, the silk items didn't disguise much. She slipped her arms into the sleeves and pulled the shirt over her shoulders. Immediately, she was assailed by the scent of Chase—his mint after-shave and the tang of male sweat. Her nipples tightened beneath her damp bra and tension collected at the juncture of her thighs. She looked up at him. "Better?" The question came out sounding like a throaty invitation to share more than lunch.

Chase stared at her, his gaze tortured. "Not a hell of a lot, but I don't know what else to do short of tying myself to my horse." He tossed the sandwiches and canteen to the ground and hooked his hands at his beltline. "We're either going to have to do something about this or I'll have to put you on a plane very soon."

Desire had turned her into a temptress. "And which would you rather do?"

He made a noise deep in his throat and pulled her to her feet. His mouth came down hard on hers and his tongue thrust forcefully, claiming her. The blood sang in her ears and desire pounded through her. His tongue probed deeper, and he wrenched open the cup of her nursing bra to capture her breast in his calloused hand. He kneaded her soft flesh with the experienced touch she'd craved that night they'd spent together in the truck, the forbidden touch she'd dreamed of for months afterward. Then he released her and backed away, panting. "Does that answer your question?"

She brought a hand to her lips. He'd nearly bruised her mouth with the force of his kiss. That night in the truck he'd never come close to being that rough, but then he'd never been pushed to the brink of frustration, either. She understood the forces that drove him to kiss her that way. They were the same forces that made her relish his demands.

He shook his head, his voice husky. "I knew that bringing you on this ride would be a temptation, but I thought I'd handle it better than this. I didn't realize how maddening it would be for us to be alone and yet . . . not alone."

"No, we're not alone."

He leaned down to retrieve the canteen and bag of sandwiches. "Well, we lugged food all the way out here. If we don't eat it, Belinda will be highly insulted."

"Then let's eat." She refastened the cup of her bra and lowered herself, still shaking, to the smooth tree root. They sat on opposite sides of the sleeping baby while they ate. Chase didn't seem in a hurry to reopen the conversation, and she didn't know where to begin with all the questions swirling in her head.

"Chase?"

He swallowed a mouthful of food and looked at her.

"I don't know what comes next. Where we go from here."

He regarded her with a steady, yet heated gaze. "I have some ideas we might be able to live with."

"Such as?" Her mouth was dry with anticipation.

"I can't expect you to give up your career and life back in New York, and I'm stuck out here for the time being, but you could schedule trips out to Arizona as often as possible. I'd want to help you with expenses, especially all the traveling."

She started to tell him that was ridiculous and he held up his hand.

"I know you don't need my money. That you're even afraid it comes with strings attached. That's not true." He gave her a wry smile. "Okay, one string. I'd want to share your bed when you came out."

A new wave of heat washed over her. "What . . . what would I tell people about all these trips I'd be taking?"

He was very quiet. "You could try the truth," he said at last.

She struggled with that concept. It would be tough facing her family and friends and explaining that she'd lied about the sperm donor when in fact her lover in Arizona was the father of her child. The whole truth would have to include that Bartholomew had been conceived in the bunk of an 18-wheeler. Her best friends would stick by her, but her parents . . . she shuddered to think how they'd react to that story, and to their grandson after they'd heard it. But maybe it was time to come clean. Maybe—

"Or not," Chase said, his tone bitter and impatient.

Amanda had the feeling a door had just slammed in her face before she'd been able to see what was on the other side. "Chase, maybe—"

"I don't really care, I guess. What does it matter what everybody else thinks?"

She glanced at him and tried to gauge his sincerity, but his expression was unreadable.

"Tell them you've developed a crush on the True Love Ranch," he continued. "Or tell them you're working on a big advertising campaign for us. Tell them you come here to have an out-of-body experience. Or to get laid by a cowboy."

"Chase!"

"Too crude, Amanda? Or too close to the truth? Forget pretending you don't want to go to bed with me again. That little cat's out of the bag."

She looked away, knowing her cheeks were pink.

"That's okay, sweetheart. You can blush and be coy to your heart's content, just so you'll let me enjoy that tempting body of yours. So what do you think? Can we work something out?"

Although she didn't like the cynical tone he'd adopted, he was offering her a way to keep her reputation intact. She'd flit out to Arizona once in a while, let him be with his son, make passionate love when Bartholomew was otherwise occupied and go back to her life in New York when the vacation was over. She should love the idea. She didn't. "What if I don't like that plan?"

A hint of vulnerability shone in his eyes as his mood shifted subtly. "Consider it, Amanda. We . . . might get to know each other that way."

"Why?" His statement about never getting married jangled in her memory. "Why get to know each other?"

He held her gaze, and the light slowly died in his eyes. He turned away. "Hell, I don't know. You're not interested in someone like me, no matter what. I don't know why I keep banging my head against a stone wall. Forget it. Just agree to bring Bartholomew out a few times a year and I promise never to lay a hand on you again."

It was the exact opposite of what she'd hoped for. "That isn't—"

"Oh, I know you want me, but you hate wanting me because you don't think I'm good enough for you." He stared into space. "You've made that very clear."

She was stung by his conclusions, but she could hardly blame him for drawing them. She had rejected him before, and that rejection had carried an unspoken implication that she didn't consider him good enough. He had no way of knowing how her feelings had changed in the past two days and she wasn't sure how she could tell him now that he'd become so defensive. Swallowing a nervous lump in her throat, she chose her words carefully. "Let's back up a minute. Were you trying to say that someday, if we discovered we got along really well, we might . . . make the arrangement between us . . . permanent?"

He glared at her. "Pretty stupid idea, right? You don't even know how stupid."

"No, it's—"

"You see, I'm not good enough for you. My pedigree has some serious problems. Last night, I spent an hour on the phone, got in touch with all the people I could think of who might be able to track down my mother. No luck. I'm not surprised—this isn't the first time I've tried to locate her. Maybe she doesn't want to be found. Maybe she's going by a different name. Maybe she's even dead. She always had lots of men around, so God knows if she could identify my father in the crowd, anyway." He sneered. "There's your family history. Pretty picture, isn't it?"

Amanda's heart wrenched with remorse at her insensitivity. How she'd pounded him with questions about his family. How those questions must have hurt him. "Chase, I'm so sorry. I didn't—"

"Save it." He didn't look at her. "I was a cute little kid. I always got into foster homes real easy. Some kids didn't."

"How . . . old were you?"

"When Mom checked out?" He picked up a stone and examined it as if it were the Hope diamond. "Three."

Three. Not even able to read. Barely able to understand what was happening. But understanding enough. Her chest tightened in grief. "How many foster homes?"

"I lost track after the first six." He threw the stone in a long arc. It landed in the pond with a loud plop and sent out ripples that made the reeds on the far shore dance. "Doesn't matter, anyway. Some were nice, some weren't so nice. They just all kind of ran together after awhile."

She didn't realize she was crying until a tear dropped onto her sandwich wrapping. Maybe before she'd had Bartholomew she wouldn't have been stabbed with so sharp a pain at the idea of a little kid left to fend for himself. But now she could hardly stand the thought. She wiped at her damp cheeks and gazed at his rigid profile.

"You're pretty quiet over there, Amanda. Guess you're about to pack up the kid and hightail it back to New York." He turned to her. "Right? You—Aaw, hell!" He stormed to his feet and towered over her. "I can take just about anything you have to dish out, babe, except pity."

"It's not pity! I feel terrible about hounding you for details of your family, when you—"

"And in my book, that adds up to you feeling sorry for me," he cut in, scowling down on her. "Spare me, little rich girl. I can do without your tears!"

Bartholomew began to cry.

"How about his tears?" She scooped him up and got to her feet. All sense of control and decorum had left her. "If you're so eager to be a daddy, how about taking care of a crying kid, huh? You woke him up with all your blustering about pity, so take some pity on this little baby, who didn't ask for any of this and was only trying to get a little sleep!"

Chase stared at her, his expression thunderous as Bartholomew's cries grew louder. Then his gaze dropped to the squalling infant in her arms and the anger drained from his face. When he spoke, his voice was hoarse but gentle. "Yeah, none of this is his fault. Come here, little guy."

She was surprised that he took the baby, but she loosened her hold and allowed Chase to lift him from her arms.

"Hey, Bartholomew," Chase murmured, cuddling the baby against his bare chest. "Take it easy, buddy. We'll work it out."

Bartholomew's cries slowed.

"That's it, buddy. Listen, kid. Bartholomew's a pretty long name for such a little guy. How about if I call you Bart instead?"

The baby snuffled and rubbed his nose against Chase's shoulder.

Amanda looked at them and her heart cracked down the middle. "I'll be glad to bring him to Arizona as often as I can," she whispered in a broken voice.

Chase glanced at her, his gaze impersonal. "Good. Because you may not need me, but he does."

I need you, too, she thought. He probably wouldn't believe her.

"Now that we have that settled, it might be better if you catch a plane out of here tonight and give us both a chance to cool down a little before we see each other again."

She could barely speak around the lump in her throat. "I suppose you're right."

After a brief moment of eye contact, Chase returned his attention to his son. "Hey, Bart, when was the last time you went fishing? Come on and I'll show you some big ones." He turned and started walking toward the pond. "Once you can hold a fishing pole, buddy, we'll have some great times up here, you and me. Early morning's good. You like to get up early? I do."

Amanda clutched her stomach and sank onto a rock. Chase and Bartholomew made an idyllic picture down by the lake—the tanned muscular father crouched by the shore balancing his tiny son on his denim-clad knee. Bartholomew waved his arms and gurgled at the sun striking sparks on the surface of the water. Such a beautiful picture. And just like that, Chase had shut her out of it.

THEY DIDN'T TALK MUCH as they packed up and headed toward the ranch. Amanda couldn't think of anything to say that wouldn't be misinterpreted as pity for Chase's childhood. She hadn't agreed to his proposal of regular visits right away because she was beginning to think she wanted more from this relationship. Apparently, he'd thought her hesitation meant she didn't want to have anything at all to do with him, and he'd shut down his feelings for her.

He'd probably had a lot of practice cutting himself off emotionally from people, she thought as they rode in silence. That skill would be a requirement for anyone being jerked from one foster home to another. And she'd had the nerve to whine because her father hadn't been as loving as she would have liked. Chase probably would have been willing to trade places with someone like her any day.

The long ride back to the ranch gave her a lot of time to think, and her thoughts weren't cheerful ones. She cringed at the knowledge that at one time, she'd been ready to deprive Chase of his son, the bundle riding trustingly like a little papoose on his back as they made their way down the canyon. She'd awakened to the realization that to take a man's child away would be unfair in most cases, but particularly unfair to a man who'd never had any family. She could see now that he'd avoided connections because he didn't believe people would honor those connections. Which would make him all the more determined to honor his to this child he'd fathered. Somehow she would keep her part of the bargain and bring father and son together as often as possible, no matter what the cost to her own aching heart. She feared she was falling in love with a man who didn't believe it could happen.

They were about a mile from the house when they heard the siren.

Chase straightened in his saddle and Bartholomew's eyes snapped open. "Amanda!" Chase called back to her. "Do you see smoke?"

"No!" Her heart began to race. She didn't know the people at the ranch well, but in the short time she'd been there, she'd come to care very much what happened to them. "What could be wrong?"

"I don't know. I hope it's not Dexter." His voice was tight with worry. "Listen, I can't ride any faster than this with the baby on my back, but you can. Go on ahead. Maybe they need an extra hand with whatever's happening. I'll be there as soon as I can."

She didn't need any more urging. Digging her heels into Pussywillow's ribs, she leaned forward and clucked her tongue at the little mare. Pussywillow shot ahead of Chase. Amanda anchored her hat on her head with one hand and moved as one with the galloping horse. She'd never wish problems on anyone at the ranch house, not even that pesky Ry McGuinnes, but oh, it was glorious to have a legitimate reason to ride full tilt up the lane. The bonds of responsibility that had begun to chafe her soul loosened temporarily, and she longed to shout with the joy of release.

CHASE WATCHED in amazement as Amanda hurtled down the road ahead of him as if she'd been launched from a slingshot. He hadn't taken her comments about her riding skills very seriously, but he could see now that the woman was a natural. Why she'd chosen to spend her life in a stuffy office when she could ride like that was beyond him.

The whine of the siren died down, and he figured whatever the emergency vehicle was, it was sitting in front of the ranch house right now. God, he hoped it wasn't Dexter. Belinda swore he'd outlast them all, especially because he walked all the way to the main road every day to get the mail. "That's more walking than any of the rest of you cowboys get," Belinda often said. "And he's eating chicken while you stuff down the steak. His heart's in great shape." Chase sure hoped so. He'd broken one of his cardinal rules and allowed himself to grow very fond of old Dex.

Yet when he trotted Mikey up to the front of the ranch house, paramedics were loading someone into the back of a Rural-Metro ambulance. And Belinda was climbing in after the stretcher.

Heart thudding with dread, Chase nudged Mikey into a trot and arrived at the back of the ambulance before the paramedics closed the doors. "Belinda?"

She turned, her eyes bright with unshed tears.

Chase had to work to get the words out. "Is it his heart?"

Belinda shook her head. "They don't think so. They think it's something he ate."

"Stomach hurts!" Dexter bellowed from inside the ambulance.

"What the hell?" Chase peered at Belinda.

Belinda swallowed. "The paramedics think we all have . . . food poisoning."

"Excuse us," said a paramedic as he closed the back doors of the ambulance and blocked Chase's view of Belinda and Dexter. "We need to get going."

Food poisoning? Chase stared after the ambulance as it started out of the driveway, red dome-lights whirling. Belinda ran a spotless kitchen. She boasted that the board of health sent restaurant owners to see her if they couldn't figure out how to keep their facilities clean, and Chase personally knew of a time a restaurant owner had come out to the True Love for that very purpose.

Maybe Dexter had some other problem, Chase thought as he dismounted by the hitching post where Pussywillow was tethered. Amanda was nowhere in sight. After tying Mikey's reins to the post, Chase adjusted the shoulder straps on the cradleboard and started toward the house. A stepladder stood on the porch, and a strand of tiny white lights hung from the rafters, as if someone had been stapling the lights across the length of the porch and had taken a break.

Inside, the main room was deserted, as well as the patio. Chase glanced into the dining room and found a sight he'd never seen before. Dirty dishes from lunch remained on the tables at nearly two in the afternoon. That never happened. The whole place had a ghost-town feel about it.

"Amanda!"

She appeared from his right, coming from the hall that led to the guest rooms. "Chase, thank God you're here! Everyone has food poisoning."

"Everyone?"

"Except Belinda, because she was too busy to eat lunch. At least that's how the paramedics diagnosed the situation. I called the board of health and someone's coming out to test the food that was served, but the symptoms are typical—stomach cramps, vomiting. Belinda called an ambulance for Dexter because she didn't want to take any chances, and because she feels so responsible, I guess. That kitchen is her whole identity."

"I know."

"Here." She walked around behind him. "Let me help you with the cradleboard and I'll tend to Bartholomew while you call Duane down at the stables."

Chase lifted the straps over his arms as Amanda relieved him of the weight of the board and Bartholomew. "Are the hands all sick, too?"

"Freddy doesn't think they will be because they didn't eat the same thing for lunch that people at the main house did. And somebody has to finish cleaning and decorating for the wedding tomorrow."

Chase turned back toward her. "Are you feeling okay? Our lunch came out of that kitchen, too."

She'd laid the cradleboard on a leather sofa to unlace it. She glanced up into his eyes and looked away again just as quickly. "I'm fine, but it's nice of you to ask."

It had been his first thought. His second had been that if she got sick, she might pass the problem on to Bart through her breast milk. But her welfare had been his first thought. The realization stunned him.

"I guess the sandwiches we took didn't have anything in them that was contaminated," she said as she pulled a wiggling Bartholomew out of his swaddling blanket. "Unless you're feeling sick?"

Not from the food, he thought. "No, I'm fine, too. I guess we shouldn't feel lucky, but I'm glad we weren't here for lunch. So everybody's down and out?"

"Everybody." Amanda stood and held Bart against her shoulder. "Freddy asked me to go check on the wedding guests for her, because she and Ry are in no condition to do it. I'd just finished making sure nobody wanted a doctor when you called to me."

"How about Leigh?"

"Leigh seems to be hit pretty bad. Apparently, she stuffed herself at lunch, claiming she had to keep up her strength for all the decorating. Even the maids and the handymen are done for. They all went home. The paramedics seem to think everyone will be okay in the morning, but we can't wait until then to finish the work. It's up to you, me, Duane and the rest of the hands."

"Then I'd better go call him." Another mysterious disaster, Chase thought as he headed for Freddy's office. He wondered if Eb Whitlock had been around today. Later he'd ask. He couldn't believe that Belinda would be behind something like this, but Duane had been spared the ordeal. Chase wondered if that was a bit too convenient. Then again, maybe this was just an accident. Everyone had been busy getting ready for the wedding. Maybe Belinda's quality control had slipped slightly, just enough to allow something in the kitchen to spoil.

Chase picked up the phone and dialed the number for the corrals. The main goal was to get ready for the wedding. It was the least he could do for Ry and Freddy. Then he realized that Amanda had sounded as if she planned to pitch in with everyone else. It looked as if she wouldn't be getting on a plane tonight, after all.

10

A REPRIEVE. Amanda wasn't sure what that would mean.
Perhaps nothing at all. But the food-poisoning incident
made it important for her to stay through tonight, and
no one would expect her to leave first thing in the morning when the wedding was taking place. The soonest
she'd be expected to fly out would be in the evening, after the reception. In the meantime, maybe she could find
a way to convince Chase that she was no longer the snob
that had stepped off the plane two days ago.

She and Chase divided up the duties. Because of her
advertising and artistic background, Amanda volunteered to supervise three of the hands in completing the
decorating of the patio and front porch. Chase would
take the other four, including Duane, and direct them in
the cleaning.

"It may not be up to Rosa's standards," Chase said,
"but we'll get the worst of it."

The afternoon passed quickly. Chase brought the infant seat over from the cottage so Amanda could set
Bartholomew in the shade while she moved around the
patio with a critical eye. Chloe appeared soon after
Amanda settled Bartholomew into the carrier and lay
beside it, as if resuming her duties.

Amanda thought of the close bond between Dexter
and the dog. She crouched and scratched behind Chloe's
ears. "Dexter will be okay, Chloe," she murmured. "He'll
be back soon."

The dog thumped her tail on the flagstone and looked up at Amanda with soulful eyes.

"I think Bartholomew needs a dog like you," Amanda said. Then she wondered how on earth she'd accomplish that. Pets were banned in her apartment building.

Curtis, a tall blond cowboy who was one of the three assigned to Amanda, sauntered toward her. "What do you want us to do first, ma'am?" he asked.

"I guess we'll finish stringing the lights." She stood, and in the process noticed Curtis casting an appreciative eye over her figure. She couldn't imagine what he found to look at. Her clothes were rumpled from her ride up the canyon, and she hadn't done anything with her hair except tie it back with the silk scarf. Her makeup was nonexistent by now. Yet Curtis seemed entranced.

With a mental shrug she turned her attention to the work at hand. "Let's start over there at the far end of the patio," she said.

Curtis motioned to the other two cowboys, Rusty and Jack, and the work commenced.

Amanda liked the Mexican-fiesta motif that Freddy and Ry had planned to execute with tiny lights, large paper flowers and several colorful *piñatas*. When it came time to stuff the *piñatas* prior to hanging them, Amanda had to keep a close eye on Rusty and Jack to make sure they didn't eat too much candy while they worked. Curtis followed Amanda around with more devotion than Chloe had shown to Bartholomew. And although Curtis was handsome in a lean sort of way, Amanda felt not a twinge of attraction. That didn't seem to penetrate Curtis's romantic fog. In his eagerness to help, he accidentally stepped on one empty *piñata*, smashing it before its time.

Eventually, the patio was finished to Amanda's satisfaction. The folding tables and chairs were in place, each with a pottery *luminaria* anchoring a scarlet tablecloth. The paper flowers bloomed in several large baskets, and the *piñatas* danced in the breeze, ready for the moment when someone would swing a baseball bat at them and spill the contents onto the flagstone beneath. When darkness arrived, the area would wink with thousands of white lights.

Amanda picked up the infant seat with Bartholomew in it. He'd begun to squirm and make little mewling sounds that told her it was nearly time for him to nurse. "Okay, guys. Let's take a break," she said. "I'll meet you on the front porch in twenty minutes so we can finish up that area, and then we'll be done."

"I'll carry the baby for you, ma'am," Curtis volunteered. "Just tell me where you're aiming to take him."

"Thanks, but it's nearly his suppertime," Amanda said.

"Oh." Curtis flushed. "Then let me get the door for you." He opened the French door into the main room of the house.

She had to assume word had gotten around the ranch that she and Chase weren't formalizing their relationship and she was therefore a free agent. That would be the only explanation for Curtis's obvious interest, considering Chase was his boss. "Thanks, Curtis," she said, choosing not to smile and encourage him any further.

"You're welcome, ma'am." Curtis touched the brim of his hat. "I'll see you on the front porch in a little bit."

"Right." She turned and walked into the room to be greeted by the sight of Chase, his legs planted apart, his fists on his hips and his expression grim beneath a hat pulled dangerously low over his eyes. The effect of outraged manhood was marred slightly by the feather duster he clutched in one big hand. Amanda pressed her lips together to keep from smiling.

"What's Curtis so chummy about?" Chase asked.

"He's a polite cowboy, that's all." Amanda took Chase's show of jealousy as a promising sign. He couldn't be jealous if he'd shut off all his feelings for her.

"The way he looked at you as he closed the door was a darn sight more than polite, if you ask me."

"I didn't," she snapped, but his possessiveness felt wonderful. "Now, if you'll excuse me, I need to find a private place to nurse Bartholomew."

At that moment, Duane came into the room pulling a canister vacuum cleaner by the hose. The cord and plug snaked out behind. "I done the hall." Duane waved the hose, to which was attached the slim tool used to clean crevices and baseboards. Amanda wondered what he could have accomplished using that narrow attachment. Duane shifted his chaw of tobacco to the other side of his lower lip. "What's next?"

Chase glanced around, looking somewhat bewildered. "Everything, I guess." He made a wide sweep with the feather duster that took in the entire main room.

Amanda bit the inside of her cheek to keep from laughing and wished she had a camera. The picture of her big, tough cowboy waving a feather duster through the air was priceless.

"If you say so." Duane located an outlet and pulled the plug toward him as if reeling in a fish hand over hand. He shoved the plug into the outlet and the vacuum surged to life. Apparently, he felt using the on-off switch was wasted labor. Stooping down, he swung the crevice attachment across the tiled floor as if it were a metal detector.

Amanda glanced at Chase, who shrugged. Shaking her head, she walked over to him. "Hold Bartholomew for a minute."

Chase stuck the handle of the feather duster in his back pocket and accepted the infant seat.

Amanda turned and approached Duane. "Can I make a suggestion?" When he didn't respond, she raised her voice. "Duane?"

"Huh?" He glanced up.

"Can I make a suggestion?"

Duane grinned, showing tobacco-stained teeth. "Shore!"

"Let's turn off the machine first!"

"Oh! Shore!" He grabbed the cord and yanked the plug from the wall in the same motion he might have used to tighten the noose on a steer's horns.

Amanda winced but said nothing about the wear and tear on the plug. This would probably be Duane's only experience with this vacuum cleaner. "Your method is great, but I'll bet there's a special attachment for these floors somewhere," she began.

Duane took off his battered hat and scratched his head. "This here's the one that was on it. You mean there's another one?"

"Probably several more."

"I'll be hornswoggled." Duane repositioned his hat on his head. "What do you make of that, Chase?"

"It's not my area."

"Mine, neither," Duane agreed.

Amanda controlled her amusement with difficulty as she turned to Chase. "If you'll show me where the cleaning supplies are kept, maybe I can find the other attachments."

"Okay. It's a storeroom just past the kitchen. I'll go with you."

"What d'ya want me to do in the meantime, Chase?" Duane asked.

Chase held the infant seat firmly in one arm as he reached behind him for the feather duster. He tossed it end over end to Duane.

Duane caught it by the feathers and nearly choked on the black cloud of dust that flew out. "What do I do with this?"

Chase paused. "Use your imagination," he said finally.

On the way through the dining room to the kitchen, Amanda could no longer control her chuckles. "You guys don't know the first thing about cleaning this place, do you?"

Chase looked offended. "Sure we do."

"What were you using the feather duster for?"

He hesitated. "To sweep out the fireplace?"

Amanda nearly choked on her laughter. "Is that an answer or a question?"

"It worked," he said with an air of injured pride.

"I imagine it did." She stifled a giggle.

"Well, I sure couldn't handle the decorating part, and you couldn't do everything, so—"

"Chase, you're doing a fine job," she said, suddenly contrite. "We're all managing the best we can, under the circumstances. By the way, I saw you talking to the inspector from the health department. What did she say?"

"It was the chicken soup."

"You're kidding." She held the swinging kitchen door open wide enough to accommodate Chase and Bartholomew in the infant seat. "Chicken soup is supposed to cure what ails you."

"I know, but somehow Belinda brewed up a toxic batch. Everybody here had some. Belinda's famous for her chicken soup. She was planning to take a kettle of it down to the bunkhouse to feed the hands, but she didn't get around to it."

"Lucky for us," said a cowboy wearing a tea towel around his waist as he worked over a sinkful of suds. Nearby, a man with his stomach sagging over his belt buckle wielded a drying towel. Amanda had never seen kitchen help wearing Stetsons, but the men seemed to know what they were doing.

"That's Ernie up to his elbows in dishwater," Chase said by way of introduction. "The guy drying is Davis."

Davis nodded. "Ma'am." Then he turned to Chase. "This food poisoning's going on the True Love's record. Think that's going to hurt business?"

"Let's hope not," Chase said.

"Ernie here's been telling me about the True Love Curse," Davis continued. "Guess I missed that story somewhere along the way, but it sure seems like the ranch has had a mess of accidents lately."

"The True Love Curse?" Amanda glanced at Chase. "What's that?"

"An old wives' tale, most likely," Chase said, sending a quelling glance in Davis's direction. "You know how superstitions get started. Come on, let's get those attachments for Duane."

"Okay. Nice to meet you both." She surveyed the clean dishes stacked on a large cutting board. One counter was filled with recently washed champagne flutes. "Keep up the good work."

Chase inclined his head toward the flutes. "I told them to get those out and clean them."

"Great idea," Amanda said as they started down the hall toward the storeroom.

Chase grinned, flashing his dimple. "You mean I'm good for something?"

She caught her breath. She loved his smile, she realized, and she hadn't seen it nearly enough in the past two days. "You're good for many things," she said.

"Oh, really?" His voice sounded a little richer, a little deeper.

Her heartbeat accelerated. "Really."

"This door on the left is the storeroom."

She opened it, found the light switch on the right wall next to the door and walked in. He came in behind her. She heard the door close as she walked over to a shelf of cleaning supplies. The scent of lemon oil permeated the windowless room, lined with shelves on all sides. Enticed by the privacy of the tiny space, she searched for the vacuum attachments with trembling hands. From behind her came a sound that could have been Chase setting the infant seat on the floor. Or it could have been Chase bumping his elbow against something on one of the shelves.

He came up behind her, too close to have Bartholomew still in his arms. "Care to expand on that last statement?"

She turned, a vacuum attachment clutched in each hand. "Where's Bartholomew?"

"Stuffed him in the mop bucket."

She gasped.

"No, I didn't. Good grief, Amanda." Chase swung aside to give her a glimpse of Bartholomew sitting in his infant seat on the tiled floor. "Seems to be having a great time examining his feet. He's fine." He turned back to her and his gaze traveled over her face. "You, on the other hand, have a large smudge on your nose."

She started to reach up with the back of her hand and he caught her wrist.

"Let me." He brushed at her nose with two fingers, then chuckled as he looked at his soot-blackened hands. "Now your nose is really dirty."

She remembered that soft chuckle, remembered the sound of it in her ear as he'd made love to her in the truck cab where they'd found themselves literally bouncing off the walls. "I always did have trouble keeping my nose clean," she said.

He looked deep into her eyes. "Especially with jokers like me around." He reached out and grasped the shelf behind her head with both hands, imprisoning her between his outstretched arms. His lips curved in a lazy smile. "I have to admit I hated it when Curtis looked at you like he was ready to take a bite."

She lifted her face to his. "You did?"

"'Fraid so. It doesn't speak well for my character, does it?" He leaned closer and his breath feathered her lips.

"Curtis means nothing to me."

"But someday, some guy in New York might look at you that way, and he might mean something." His lips hovered nearer; his eyes were half-closed. "I've never allowed myself to be jealous of anyone before. Now I can't seem to help it." His voice roughened. "God, Amanda, you're tearing me apart."

The vacuum attachments clattered to the floor. "Then let me put you back together, cowboy," she whispered, sliding her hands along his beard-stubbled jaw and bringing his mouth down to meet hers.

He groaned as she slipped her tongue between his teeth and stroked the roof of his mouth. Nipping and teasing his lips, she reached down and snapped open the fasteners of his shirt so she could run her hands over his chest.

"I hope you know what you're starting," he murmured against her mouth.

"I have a general idea." Stroking down over the pewter chain, she tunneled her fingers through his wiry chest hair and scratched her fingernails lightly over his hard nipples. His chest heaved and he deepened the kiss. Amanda opened to him, inviting him to delve into the moist recesses of her mouth. Inviting him to dare yet more.

When she reached down to the fly of his jeans and stroked him there, the contents of the shelf he was clutching began to rattle.

He wrenched his mouth from hers with obvious effort and stared down at her, his eyes glittering, his breath coming in great gasps. "You were supposed to be on a plane by now."

She rubbed the heel of her hand over the bulge in his jeans. "Is that what you want?"

He stared at her for what seemed like forever. Finally, his answer came, low and full of tension. "I want you to leave your door unlocked tonight."

She trembled, her body already heavy with need. "All right."

"And snap up my shirt. If I do it, I'll leave soot marks everywhere and people will think I've been massaging my own chest in here."

Triumph and desire surged through her as she refastened his shirt with slow, sensuous motions, taking time to caress him as she did so.

"Amanda, you're taking a big chance, playing around like that. You're liable to end up on your back on this concrete floor with soot marks all over that white skin of yours."

Holding his shirtfront with both hands, she stood on tiptoe to brush his lips with hers. "I just don't want you to forget to come by tonight. For my bedtime story, you can tell me about the True Love Curse."

He made a sound deep in his throat. "I have a slightly different bedtime story in mind." He leaned down and ravished her lips once more before pushing away from the shelf with a resigned sigh. "We'd better get out there before Duane uses the feather duster on the white drapes."

Amanda's eyes widened. "Would he?"

Chase's mouth curved in a smile. "Well, I told him to use his imagination. Duane is a good old boy, but he has the imagination of a hubcap."

"Judging from that night in the truck, that's not one of your shortcomings."

"And I was working in a limited space, too."

She caught her breath as erotic images assaulted her.

"Don't give me that look, you devil woman. As it is, I'll have to stagger out of here bowlegged." He leaned down and scooped the vacuum attachments from the floor. "I'm taking these to Duane. This might be the most private place to feed Bart, if you want to stay. There's a folding stool in the corner."

"Are you coming back?"

"Knowing you're in here with your blouse undone? Not likely." His eyes took on a wicked gleam. "Shall I tell Curtis you'll be a little later than you thought coming out to the porch?"

She put a hand to her throat, where her pulse was beating madly. She'd completely forgotten about the rest of the decorating job. Completely forgotten about Curtis and his hopeless crush. A smile of feminine delight touched her lips as she realized that was exactly what Chase had intended. "Please," she said.

"Shall I tell him why you'll be a little late?"

"I doubt that will be necessary. I've discovered nothing's a secret for long around here."

Chase stood with his hand on the doorknob as his gaze raked her possessively. "Good."

11

CHASE MOVED through the rest of the cleaning and decorating in a daze. Freddy, Ry, Leigh and the wedding guests kept to their rooms and couldn't be tempted to come out for the makeshift dinner, which consisted of peanut butter and jelly sandwiches washed down with beer. None of the hands complained. Chase figured it was because peanut butter wasn't known for giving anyone food poisoning. During the meal, Belinda called from the hospital and said Dexter was better but the doctor wanted to keep him overnight. They'd be back first thing in the morning.

After dinner, Chase sent Amanda back to the cottage with Chloe as escort while he and the hands tidied up. Then he walked with them out to the front porch just as the last russet glow was fading from the sky. "Thanks, guys," he said.

"You're shore welcome," Duane said as he started down the flagstone walkway to the rusty pickup he'd used to haul the hands up from the bunkhouse. Then he turned and grinned at Chase. "'Course, you know my dang manicure is ruined."

Davis sashayed up beside him, flung an arm around his shoulders and spoke in falsetto. "You should use rubber gloves, dear. I always do, and it keeps my hands so nice."

"I wanna know why I didn't get to wear an apron with ruffles," Ernie complained. "I always liked aprons with ruffles."

"I'll get you one for Christmas," Curtis said. "Red-and-white-striped, to match your eyes."

Laughing and trading insults, the cowboys piled into the back of Duane's pickup.

Just before he drove off, Duane leaned out the window of the truck. "I used to think that high-dollar woman of yours was a waste of your time," he said. "But she's okay. Purty little filly, too." Duane beeped the horn and drove away.

A high-dollar woman. Good description, Chase thought. He had a feeling Amanda was going to be very expensive indeed, and the cost would have nothing whatsoever to do with money.

Fifteen minutes later he was showered, shaved, dressed and on his way through the patio when a voice called from the shadows.

"What's your hurry, cowboy?"

Chase spun around and saw Ry lying on a chaise longue. "Hey. You scared the crud out of me. Feeling any better?"

"Some. I was getting cabin fever in my room."

Chase walked back toward the chaise, a smile tugging at his mouth. "And bridegroom jitters?"

"How should I know?" Ry grumbled. "I expect bridegroom jitters and food poisoning feels about the same."

"I wouldn't know. Never had either one. Never plan to."

"Yeah, you're such a free man you can hardly wait to get over to that little cottage."

"Uh..."

"Don't try to get high and mighty with me, Lavette. You're as lovestruck as I am. If Amanda offered to stay at the True Love and wash your socks for the rest of your life, you'd jump at the chance."

Chase adjusted his hat and looked away. "Yeah, well, I can guarantee she's not gonna do that, buddy."

Ry laughed. "You're not giving yourself much credit. The night's still young."

"That's not what I'm looking for, going over there."

"You're not looking for sex?"

"That's *all* I'm looking for." Chase thought it sounded good, just the sort of thing the old Chase would have said. But the old Chase was fast disappearing in the force of this driving passion. "The last time was a one-night stand for her. Now it's my turn," he added, as if smart remarks could stop the momentum of his downward slide into neediness. Fat chance.

Ry chuckled. "If you say so." Then his voice lost its playful tone. "What do you make of this food-poisoning business?"

Chase hooked his thumbs in his belt loops. "Could somebody deliberately cause something like that?"

"I don't know why not. Just drop some tainted chicken in the kettle. It could have been anyone who had access to the kitchen."

"Which was damn near everybody, today," Chase said. "Was Whitlock over here?"

"I don't think so. But did you notice who didn't eat any soup?"

"Yeah, but come on, Ry. Belinda wouldn't poison her own husband."

"How do you know he was poisoned? Those two old people are crafty. She could have coached him on how to react."

Chase shook his head. "I just can't buy it. I saw her face just before she got in the ambulance. You know, Duane didn't eat any soup, either. None of the hands did, for that matter. Maybe somebody has a grudge you don't even know about."

Ry heaved a sigh. "Anything's possible. Damn, but I hate having these suspicions."

"Davis mentioned something today about a 'True Love Curse.' What's that all about?"

"That's more Leigh's department than mine, but the way I heard it, some cavalrymen killed a village of Indian women and children on this spot back in the 1800s. The men of the tribe supposedly put a curse on the land and said no white man would ever profit from it."

Chase gazed uneasily at the shadowy mountains towering above the ranch house. "Did you hear this before we bought the place?"

"Yeah, but I don't believe in superstition, so I didn't see the point in repeating the story to you and Gilardini. We may have a problem on the True Love, but it sure as hell isn't on account of some century-old curse. It's because some flesh-and-blood trickster wants to drive us off of this land. I just wish I could catch somebody in the act."

"I think you should forget it for tonight, buddy, and try to get some rest. Tomorrow's your big day."

"And what if someone tries to ruin that, too?"

Chase couldn't very well promise there wouldn't be any accidents on Ry's wedding day. "Let's just hope our friends outnumber our enemies tomorrow," he said, turning to go. "See you in the morning, bridegroom."

"Yeah. Good luck tonight, cowboy."

Chase raised a hand in acknowledgment of the remark. He didn't comment that a guy who didn't believe in superstitions shouldn't be wishing anyone good luck, either. As he walked toward the cottage, a pewter sliver of moon hung in the western sky with Venus dangling off its tip like a diamond pendant. He'd wished on a star exactly once. Nothing had happened. After that, he'd relied on himself to get what he wanted. And if he couldn't get it, then he'd convince himself it wasn't worth having.

No light shone from the cottage windows, and his heart beat faster. She was already in bed. Waiting. Or else she'd changed her mind, locked the door and turned out the light to warn him away.

In the pale gleam from the crescent moon, he could make out Chloe stationed outside the door on the porch, instead of inside the cottage. That was a promising development. Chloe stood and wagged her tail as Chase drew near.

"Come here, girl," Chase called softly. Chloe trotted down the steps toward him and shoved her nose against the palm of his hand. He scratched behind her ears and lifted her muzzle to look into her eyes. "Go find Ry," he commanded. "You stay with Ry tonight. I'll be on duty here." Chloe whined. "Go find Ry," Chase said again. The black-and-white dog bounded down the moonlit path to the main house.

Chase stepped up on the porch, wondering if Amanda could hear the sound of his boots on the weathered pine above the soft purr of the air-conditioning unit. He held his breath and turned the knob.

It opened.

He stood in the doorway, his heart hammering, as his eyes adjusted to the darkness. There was music, unfamiliar music with violins, playing on the radio. Gradually, like a Polaroid picture developing, the four-poster came into focus with its expanse of lace-edged sheets.

And there, reclining against a mound of fluffy pillows, the sheet pulled up over her breasts, her shoulders bare and her glorious hair spread around her, was Amanda. His throat went dry.

"The baby?" His question came out as a feeble rasp.

"Stuffed him in a mop bucket," she murmured in a low voice.

"I see."

"I hope you don't mind the music. It helps him sleep."

"No." He'd listen to somebody with a pocket comb and a kazoo if he could make love to Amanda while it was playing. He was a country-and-western fan, himself, but this music seemed to suit Amanda. Unwilling to abandon the sight of her stretched out in bed, Chase reached behind him to close and lock the door. Then he took off his hat and sailed it toward a bedpost. It caught and spun around once, almost in time to the music, before settling there.

"Good aim."

"I've practiced."

She muffled her laughter against her hand.

He walked toward the bed, unfastening his shirt as he came. "I figured that any cowboy worth his spurs should be able to do that before he climbs into a four-poster bed with a woman." His arousal pushed painfully against his clothing.

"I agree," she said softly. "What else have you been practicing?"

"Lately? Not much." And he hoped he wouldn't pay for his lack of recent sexual activity by taking her like some rutting animal. He'd have to be careful. He wanted her so much he was beginning to shake. If he could pace himself to that gentle music, he'd be okay.

"If you tell me you've been celibate since that night in the truck, I'll know you're a liar," she said.

He leaned on the bedpost to pull off each boot in turn. "Then I won't tell you that."

"Who was she?"

He paused in the act of unhooking his belt from the buckle. In the past he would have shut down that line of questioning real quick. But that was because he'd made it a rule never to ask those same questions of the women he'd slept with. He'd already broken that rule with Amanda. He'd broken several of his rules with Amanda. "A waitress and a bartender," he said as he pulled his belt through the loops. "Very nice ladies."

"Two? At once?"

He controlled his laughter because of the baby. "Never tried that. Always thought it would be too confusing." He dug the condoms out of his pocket before he stepped out of his jeans.

"Did they... know about each other?"

"No." He walked to the head of the bed and deposited the condoms on the table beside it. "But then, they didn't ask." He was close enough to see the shine of her eyes in the dim light. Her gaze was fastened on him, and under the sheet her breasts moved up and down in time to her rapid breathing. He reached for the elastic of his briefs.

"Did you ask them if they'd had other lovers besides you?"

"No, I didn't."

She met that admission with a satisfied smile and asked no more questions. He figured she was remembering that he'd asked about other men within an hour of seeing her again. He'd told Ry he was here for a one-night stand, and the stupidity of that statement was already becoming obvious. He pushed his briefs down and released his straining erection.

Her glance swept downward, then back to his face. She caught her lower lip between her teeth and he clenched his hands to keep from flinging himself on her. The music. He had to use the rhythm of the music to stay calm. He took the sheet back slowly when he longed to rip it away from her body. The movement of the sheet stirred the scent of her perfume, which reached out to him with memories he'd never erase.

His breath came out in a long, shaky sigh and he cursed his lack of schooling. He wanted to tell her how beautiful she looked lying there naked against the white sheets, her body almost glowing, but he'd never be able to find the right words, especially when he needed her so much he couldn't think straight.

He returned his gaze to her face as he slid into bed beside her. He lay there, not touching her, just drowning in those eyes and feeling like a novice, a beginner, a virgin. His next move was too important. After loving so many women that he'd lost track of the number, he had no idea where to begin.

She took the decision away from him. Slipping a hand up the curve of his jaw, she guided him down with subtle pressure until their lips hovered a breath apart. "Get this straight, Lavette. I don't share," she whispered just before she kissed him. It was a kiss that shattered what was left of the wall he'd tried to build around his heart. It was a kiss of complete, utter surrender.

With a groan, he pressed deep into her mouth and took that surrender, burying himself in the limitless passion she offered. Now he knew what to do.

As violins teased him to even greater awareness, he found the curve of her neck with a sure touch, followed it over her shoulder, into the tender crook of her elbow, down past the delicate bend of her wrist until at last he laced his fingers through hers. That clasp of hands felt more intimate than any touch he'd ever shared with a woman. She gripped his fingers as if she'd never let go. He returned the pressure as he moved his lips to the hollow of her throat. He'd forgotten how perfectly his tongue fit there, and how she shuddered as he trailed the moist tip over her collarbone and down the slope of her breast.

He remembered the silken texture of her skin, the exotic taste of scented lotion, but this time she swelled beneath him with more urgency than before. He listened to the rhythm of the music, circling the pebbled areola slowly, making the music part of the caress. Her fingers tightened in his, and he took her nipple into his mouth.

The taste of her milk stirred him as nothing had in his life. He felt as if her essence had passed into him, bonding them in a way he'd never be able to untangle. And didn't want to. He kissed his way to her other breast, eager for her, unashamed to let her know how he craved this closeness. She moaned and tunneled the fingers of her free hand through his hair.

Memories of their long night in the truck came rushing back. He'd learned about her then, and the imprint was still fresh, as if it had been only days instead of months. He retraced the path between her breasts, heard the familiar catch in her breathing as he caressed the gentle valley between her ribs. There was a ticklish spot—his tongue found it again—that he'd loved to lick just to hear her gasp of laughter. When her laughter bubbled out on schedule, his heart rejoiced in rediscovery.

And now, the most beloved and best-remembered part of the journey, through the thicket of curls that would glow like burnished copper if he could only have light. Her musky woman-scent rose to meet him, signaling how much she wanted him, and he longed to shout his delight. Instead, he paid homage to that need in ways that made her writhe beneath him. He pinned her thighs with his forearms and settled in, his heart beating in fierce triumph as he brought cries to her lips, cries muffled against a hastily grabbed pillow.

When she began to tremble and clench beneath him, he rose, wanting the end to come when he was deep inside her. Usually adept at putting on condoms, he fumbled this time. The music filtering through the labored sound of his breathing mingled with her soft plea to hurry, hurry. Please hurry. No. He forced himself to rejoin her with exquisite slowness, in time to the music. Always in time to the music.

She lay back among the tousled pillows, her hair in disarray, her legs spread, her breath shallow. "I don't remember wanting you . . . this much." Her voice was like the sigh of wind through the leaves in Rogue Canyon.

"You didn't." He braced himself above her and took the time to comb her hair away from her face. This moment would be over soon enough. He didn't have to rush it. The music. He'd move with the music. "I didn't want you this much, then, either. We've had a long time to think about it."

She didn't deny that she'd been thinking of him all that time, and he took satisfaction from that. She might not have liked that she was obsessed with him, might have fought it with all the strength of her upper-class background, but she'd lost the fight. If she hadn't, she wouldn't be lying beneath him now, her hands reaching for his hips, wanting this union more than anything in the world.

"Wait," he whispered. He caught her hand and brought it over her head. Then he pulled her other hand there, too, and circled both wrists in the fingers of his left hand. "Let it build."

She arched like a bow, her wrists and her hips anchoring her to the bed. "Chase . . . I need you now."

"You'll need me more in a little while."

"No." She moved her head back and forth on the pillow. "I couldn't want you more than this. I feel like screaming."

"Don't." He leaned down and covered her mouth with his, but he didn't push into her, much as his aching loins begged him to. He left room for his right hand, his gearshift hand, he thought wryly, to bring her to another level of awareness. He absorbed her moans into his mouth as he fondled her breasts—cupping their weight, massaging their fullness, caressing the nipples until his fingers were sticky with milk.

He trailed his knuckles between her ribs to her navel, where he pressed gently, knowing she was sensitive there. The music surged around them, through them, as he moved the knuckle of his index finger lower, finding the jewel buried in a thicket of curls. He rubbed gently, then with more force as she lifted her hips. When she was wild with sensation, he stopped, letting her fall gradually back to earth as he kissed her.

"You are insane," she said against his mouth.

His heart thundered as if he'd just survived a pileup on the freeway. "I think you're right."

"When, Chase? When will you give me what I want?"

"Now." He thrust deep, catching her by surprise.

She gasped and her eyes flew open. He gazed down at her, wanting her to remember his face for the rest of her life. "It may never feel like this again, Amanda." He released her hands.

"Chase..."

His mouth curved. "As they say on the bumper stickers—'get in, sit down, shut up and hang on.'"

He abandoned the rhythm of the sedate music now. It was too tame for what was about to happen between them. He drew back and pushed in tight again, a movement that brought her hands to his shoulders and her nails into his skin. He didn't care. This was worth bleeding for.

His next movement was more forceful, and she bucked when he applied pressure to that tiny spot that controlled so much of her. Yes, Amanda. We might wake the baby this time. Again he came in, and again, always on target, while the momentum built in him just as surely, just as potently. Again. Oh, Amanda. He'd meant to stay in control until she crossed the line. He'd planned this all in his head—until the moment when his control snapped, and he plunged into her with a frenzy that mocked him with its power.

She rose beneath him calling his name as spasms shook her. It was all he needed to explode like a gasoline tank touched by a match. He was flying apart, yet anchored to safety, all at the same time. It was a pedal-to-the-metal ride of passion, and he'd never known anything like it.

THROUGH THE DELIRIOUS haze of pleasure that settled over Amanda in the aftermath of Chase's loving, came the soft croaking sounds of Bartholomew, waking up. It was her fault, she knew. She'd tried to be quiet, but Chase had robbed her of reason.

Chase lay against her, his chest hair causing delicious friction against her breasts, the pewter medallion making a remembered imprint on her skin.

"I have to get him," she murmured.

"I know. We woke him up."

"I did."

"I did my share of making noise," Chase said. "Want me to get him and bring him to you?"

It was a novel, beautiful concept that had never occurred to Amanda before. "Yes. Please."

Chase eased out of her, made a quick trip to the bathroom and then lifted Bartholomew from his cradle. "Hey, Bart," he crooned. "How's it going, big guy? Is the neighborhood a little rowdy for you?"

Amanda propped her head on her fist and watched them in the pale light that drifted in the window. Chase looked like a statue by Rodin as he stood silvered by moonlight. Bartholomew stopped his hiccuping little cries and seemed to study the new situation—being rescued from his bed at night by this person with a deep voice and gentle hands.

Perhaps not so gentle, Amanda thought as she remembered how he'd exacted his toll, wringing the last bit of response from her as if he wanted nothing to remain inside. Ah, but he'd miscalculated. No sooner had he left her bed than she'd begun to yearn again, and that yearning had started the cycle all over. He'd said it might never be like that again, and perhaps he was right, but she'd like to find out.

However, first there was Bartholomew to deal with. "Bring him here," she murmured.

"Want to go see Mom? I guess so. You won't find what you're looking for here."

Chase's soft laugh tickled down Amanda's spine. She was lost and she knew it. The cowboy had won her heart.

He walked over to the bed and laid Bartholomew in her arms. "He's no dummy. He knows where the good stuff is."

Right in this room, Amanda thought with a rush of emotion. *All I need to be happy is right in this room.* She nestled Bartholomew against her and gave him her breast.

Chase stood silhouetted against the window, his back to her. "That is the sweetest sound."

"What?"

"Him nursing. I love to hear it."

And babies nurse for such a short time, Amanda thought. Perhaps by the time she returned to Arizona, Bartholomew would be weaned. But she didn't say that. The moment was too perfect to spoil. She stroked her baby's head and admired the sturdy outline of his father standing at the window.

Chase turned and walked back to the bed. "I want to stay the night, Amanda."

"I expected you to."

"I wasn't sure." He eased back into bed. "You're used to your space."

"It's nice having you here." She sighed. "God, we sound so polite."

He chuckled. "Kind of silly, isn't it? One minute we're as close as two people can be, and the next we're talking like strangers who happen to be sharing a table at a crowded restaurant."

"That's because this is so backward. We made love for one night and became parents. How are two people supposed to handle that?"

"It's been confusing, all right." He trailed a finger down the side of her breast, stopping just short of her nipple, where Bartholomew was fastened, his pudgy hands pressing against the fullness. "But I wouldn't want to change any of it."

She met his gaze over the top of Bartholomew's fuzzy head, and time seemed to stop. At the moment, that was all she wanted.

12

AMANDA HAD WONDERED if Chase would be jealous of the baby's needs. Yet he lay with his chin propped on his hand and watched with an indulgent smile as she nursed Bartholomew. Then, true to his word, he helped change him, all the while holding the palm of his hand ready to deflect accidents.

"Pretty impressive equipment, Bart," he said with obvious pride as he gazed down at the naked little boy squirming on the bed between them.

"As if that's the measure of a man." Amanda fastened the adhesive tabs on the diaper and reached for the soft cotton shirt she'd laid on the bedside table.

"Hey, it's a start." Chase leaned toward the baby and whispered, "Don't let her kid you, Bart, old buddy. They all say they don't care about size and pretend it's our hang-up. But I've seen *Playgirl* magazine. They care."

Bartholomew gurgled and grabbed Chase's nose. Chase cried out in mock pain as Bartholomew crowed and tugged harder. Amanda laughed and wished she had a camera. Then she realized that she'd just had the urge to record Chase and Bartholomew together on film. If anyone saw that, one picture would be worth a thousand words.

"So you think you can lead people around by the nose?" Chase eased the baby's fingers loose. "I'll bet your mother taught you that trick." He glanced up at Amanda and gave her a wink.

"I beg your pardon." She tried to adopt his bantering tone as she popped the shirt over Bartholomew's head. But her heart was too full from watching them together.

"Then again, maybe it hasn't been my nose you've been leading me around by," he said softly, his teeth flashing white in the pale light as he smiled at her. "It might be something a bit lower. I wasn't very good at anatomy in school."

She scooped Bartholomew up and slid out of bed. "But I imagine you were very good at anatomy after school was out." She turned toward the cradle.

"No comment. But what about you, Amanda? Did you kiss the boys and make them cry?"

She adjusted the blanket in the cradle, not feeling very comfortable talking about her romantic past, or lack of it. "My story is pretty dull. You'd get bored in a heartbeat." She settled Bartholomew down on the blanket and rocked him gently with one hand.

"Try me."

"I was quiet, a bookworm. Always writing, drawing, reading. When I wasn't doing that, I was riding my horse. And I was—still am—a feminist. I saw dating and marriage as a trap for women, so I didn't aim in that direction."

"Never even engaged?"

"Once. It didn't work out." She gazed down at Bartholomew. She'd never seen him so relaxed, as if the doting attention of both parents was exactly what he needed. Gradually, his eyes drifted closed. She rocked a while longer before standing and walking back to the bed. "From the way I acted in the truck that night, you probably thought I was a real swinging chick, but I'm not. I'd never behaved that way before."

He reached out and caught her hand, drawing her back down to the bed. "That's what made you different," he murmured, curving his arm around her waist and urging her against him until they were pressed together in sweet tension. "You were scared and excited at the same time." He massaged the length of her spine as he talked. "I figured the only times you'd ever been to bed with a man were after you'd known him a long time."

"That's true." Barely tamped desire flared at his touch, sending heated signals that tightened her nipples and moistened the pulsing channel he had so recently explored. "You were an adventure," she said. "My one chance to be a naughty girl."

Chase cupped her bottom with both hands, kneading her flesh. "And was I wild enough for you?"

Her body grew languorous and willing as his erection pressed against her belly. "You were . . . very nice."

"The hell with nice." He adjusted his body to hers, positioning her so that his shaft separated the folds of her femininity. "Nice is what those other guys were, the ones you had dinner with a million times before you let them touch you like this." His movements were subtle but powerful as he eased up and down, connecting with her most sensitive spot without entering her.

She grew breathless with the mounting tension. His ability to bring her to flashpoint so quickly was unnerving. "You were incredible," she managed to say.

"So were you," he said in a gruff voice. "Inexperience isn't necessarily a bad thing."

"Chase." She gripped him urgently. "Kiss me, Chase, before I wake . . . the baby."

He muffled her cries with his mouth as a climax shattered the last of her reserve. As the quivering subsided, he moved from her lips to the curve of her ear. "Are you getting warmed up?" he whispered.

She sighed. "I think so."

"I was hoping you were. There are a few things I'd like you to do for me." Then he murmured his requests, requests that turned the blood that was already singing through her veins into molten lava. His loving had removed all shame. Rising over him, she satisfied the first of his wishes by trailing her fiery hair over him, tickling and tantalizing his chest, his inner thighs, his quivering erection. She wrapped her hair around that throbbing shaft and drew it away slowly, judging the effect by the rasp of his breathing and the clenching of his hands.

Then she used her tongue on his muscular body, laving his tanned skin until he was quivering in anticipation. His control was incredible. When she touched his shaft with the tip of her tongue, all she heard was an intake of breath—between clenched teeth. She took her time. After all, he'd asked her to. But at last she heard a muted plea of "enough."

She slid up to kiss his mouth and he rolled her to her back in a fierce embrace.

"Any more experience and you'll be dangerous," he gasped, looming over her, his eyes glittering.

She laughed softly, triumphantly, and arched her breasts upward in invitation.

With a moan he accepted the invitation, sending reverberations spiraling downward to her heated center as he sucked.

"Come to me," she begged, abandoning all modesty. "I want you inside me."

He lifted his head and gazed down at her, his breathing harsh. "I've never wanted anyone this much."

His words set off skyrockets in her head. "Neither have I. Oh, Chase, what are we going to do?"

The corner of his mouth tilted up. "I know what we're going to do right this minute." He reached for one of the condoms on the table.

Bartholomew stirred and started to cry.

Chase paused in midmotion. "Maybe not just this minute."

"I'll try rocking him." Battling her frustration, Amanda rolled to her stomach and reached for the edge of the cradle. She rocked it slowly, easing Bartholomew back into sleep. Behind her, cellophane crinkled, and she trembled just thinking of Chase sheathing himself, Chase waiting for her.

He trailed a finger down her backbone. "How's he doing?" he murmured.

"Going back to sleep." She stopped rocking as Bartholomew's breathing grew steady. At last she removed her hand from the edge of the cradle with a sigh.

"Time to go off duty for a while," Chase said. Caressing her bottom, he slipped his hand between her thighs and probed gently until he gained the entrance he sought. With deft fingers he stroked, and she unconsciously lifted herself into the caress.

His breath caught. His knee brushed hers as he moved behind her and guided her farther upward, caressing, encouraging her with soft endearments. Heart racing, body pounding with urges outside her experience, she complied, rising to her knees and offering herself in a way that reached back beyond the rules of civilization, to a time of caves, flickering fires and base needs satisfied.

When he eased into her, she gasped at the primitive carnality of the gesture. The lust of animals flowed through her, and she took her lip between her teeth to keep from crying out her fevered response. His hips tight against her buttocks, he slid his hand over her thigh and into the moist valley where her pleasure point lay. And she dimly recognized that this was the difference that separated such a basic act from the mating of animals— he would give while he took. She became sensation itself as he moved rhythmically inside her and coaxed her to greater heights with firm pressure from his fingers.

As the tempo increased, she fought to be silent, knowing from muffled groans that he waged the same war. When the moment came, she pressed her lips together and whimpered. She heard his gasp, his final, shuddering thrust, and she absorbed the pulsing impact of his climax. They trembled together for a moment before he withdrew and she sank to the cool sheets, her body sapped of the will to move.

He left the bed for only a moment, and soon he was back, lying beside her and smoothing her hair from her face.

She gave him a sated smile. "I think that qualifies as wild enough."

He smiled back, a lazy, contented smile. "Did I shock you?"

"A little."

He brushed a finger across her lower lip. "Good."

"Are you setting out to shock me?"

"I'm setting out to show you what you've been missing."

AS LONG AS the room remained dark, Amanda could allow feelings to override thoughts, touch to supplant words. But toward dawn, as objects in the room took on a sharper edge, so did the meandering of her mind. Chase dozed beside her, an arm flung over her waist. She liked the weight of it there far too much. She still had no idea if this drifter lying beside her had decided to change his wandering ways, and what it meant to her future if he had.

The passion they'd generated through the night could all be the work of an accomplished lover seducing a woman who'd lived like a nun for almost a year. Yet she suspected something far more complex had happened in the large four-poster bed. Originally, Chase had been no more than a fantasy figure, a sexy blue-collar worker willing to provide earthy, inhibition-shattering sex. But in the past two days he'd become so much more to her—a man who'd struggled against the odds to establish an identity, a father capable of incredible gentleness toward his child and a tender partner in lovemaking, a partner willing to put aside past hurts for present pleasure.

By some miracle, Chase Lavette had emerged from his unhappy background with a generous spirit. Far more generous than hers, Amanda admitted with chagrin. Yet in the warmth of Chase's arms, her reservations melted away and she began to dream of ways they could be together, all three of them. And as well, she wasn't ready to abandon the search for his family. The information was still important for Bartholomew's sake, but she thought it was important for Chase, too. Everyone had some good news in their background. She wanted to help Chase find his.

The telephone rang, startling her out of her reverie. She picked up the antique handset and answered in a muted voice.

Ry was on the other end, sounding frazzled. "Amanda? I hate like the devil to bother you this early, but is Chase there?"

The realization that everyone on the True Love would know Chase had spent the night gave her a mild shock. She wasn't used to people knowing her intimate business. "Yes, he is." She covered the mouthpiece and glanced at Chase, who lay with his head on his outstretched arm, looking at her with an unreadable expression. "It's Ry." She handed him the receiver.

Chase took it and rolled to his back, tugging the cloth-covered cord across Amanda. "This better be important, bridegroom." He turned his head to look at Amanda and noticed the spiral cord stretched across her bare breasts. With a little smile he eased the cord back and forth across her nipples, which snapped to attention at the casual contact.

How easily he demonstrated his power over her. She would have resented that power if she hadn't glanced down and noticed his penis stir and gradually stiffen as he gazed at her breasts.

"Sure, I'll do that," Chase said. "No problem. How is everyone this morning?" He drew the cord across her breast more slowly this time. "Glad to hear it. Yeah, I'll pick them up by seven and be back before eight. Don't worry, nobody wants to miss watching you get branded, buddy. See you soon." He took the receiver from his ear.

She reached for it, disappointed that he'd referred to Ry's marriage vows as "getting branded." Maybe she'd better rein in her thoughts of a close relationship with this drifter. They'd had good sex. Perhaps that was all they were to have together. "Want me to hang that up for you?"

"Not when things are becoming interesting." He propped himself on his elbow and dragged the cord over her nipple one more time. "Maybe not at all. We don't need any calls right now."

Her breathing quickened. "Don't you have to leave?"

"Not yet." He curled the cord around the fullness of her breast. "Ry needs me to pick up Belinda and Dexter at the hospital, but it's only a little after five now." He pulled the cord a little tighter and looked into her eyes. "How come the phone didn't wake up the little guy?"

"He's used to that noise, I guess." Her eyes widened as he drew the cord down between her legs. "At the apartment I get a lot of calls . . ." She gasped as he slid the cord into the cleft of her femininity. " . . . from work."

"Sounds like you needed this vacation." He laid the receiver between her legs and drew the cord gently upward, making sure each ascending spiral teased her to a higher level of arousal. Then he picked up the receiver and drew the cord down again.

She was aflame for him. "Chase, you'll get the telephone cord—"

"Wet? Looks like it."

"But the management..." She moaned as he eased the cord back down.

"I am the management, sweetheart." He pulled the cord in a little tighter. "There, that should mark my place for a minute. Don't move." He kept his gaze on her as he put on the condom. She didn't move, but her body hummed like an engine that had been started and needed only the slightest touch on the throttle to leap forward.

Then he was back, moving between her thighs, replacing the telephone cord with his fingers, but leaving the receiver beside them on the bed, off the hook. "Just where I left off," he whispered. "Good morning, sweetheart."

"Good...morning," she whispered back, arching into his caress. She'd thought this morning they'd talk, but he didn't seem to want to leave time for that.

Lifting her hips still more he slid into her effortlessly.

Through a sensuous haze she looked up into his face. Unspoken words of love trembled on her lips, words that might drive him away. After all, he wouldn't want to risk being branded like his partner Ry. "You're very good at this, cowboy," she murmured instead.

A shadow seemed to cross his expression, almost as if she'd insulted him, somehow. His jaw tensed. "You bet I am, babe," he said, his tone almost harsh. Then he loved her hard, wringing a response from her, taking his own pleasure, and leaving her feeling strangely empty. He departed the cottage with few words. Amanda stared at the closed door as tears burned her eyes and the dreams she had begun to weave hung in tatters around her.

BETWEEN BRINGING Dexter and Belinda home and helping the hands with the horses, Chase kept busy prior to the wedding. But he still had time to think and cool off a little. Amanda probably hadn't meant her remark the way it had sounded, but after she'd said it, he'd thought she saw him as just another hunk of meat, the way women had been reacting to him all his life. Not so long ago that had been okay, and had even given him bragging rights with the truckers he knew. But for the first time in his life he wanted more than sex from a woman. He wanted lovemaking. He had no practice asking for that, and it took so little to send him running for cover. Maybe sometime during the day he'd work up the courage to talk to her, really talk.

As his last chore before the wedding, he'd volunteered to drive a buggy from the corrals to the main house while Duane and the hands led the string of horses. The buggy was for Dexter and Belinda, so they could make it out to the homestead site.

When he arrived, the wedding party was milling around in the front yard, men and women separated into same-sex groups while Duane and Leigh tried to keep some order. The men wore brightly patterned western shirts, while the women had opted for broomstick skirts and fluffy blouses. All except Amanda, whose turquoise dress was probably a designer number from Fifth Avenue. She stood talking to Belinda with Bartholomew held against her shoulder.

As she turned to shade the baby from the sun, the light caught in her red hair and Chase's heart wrenched with longing. He wanted to go over and apologize for his abruptness this morning, but now wasn't the time, not with so many people around. Amanda spoke to Freddy, who moved restlessly though the crowd of women. She wore a dress of snowy lace decorated with long white fringe that danced as she walked. Ry had told him that Freddy's outfit had been modified from a dress that had belonged to her grandmother. Freddy had added a white Stetson draped with a white scarf and white lace-up granny boots.

It wasn't much of a mental stretch for Chase to imagine Amanda in bridal white, but he shoved the image aside, frightened by the unfamiliar desires it produced in him. Wanting something you might never have was dangerous.

Ry stood in the center of the group of men. He looked hot, but he'd insisted on wearing a black western jacket over his white shirt and black western-cut slacks. Love did crazy things to a man, Chase thought. Dexter stood nearby, balancing himself on his walker.

Duane's call for attention got nowhere. Finally, he hopped up on the three-foot wall surrounding the yard and whistled through his teeth. "That's more like it," he said as everyone turned in his direction. "Now, I got to tell everybody—you're responsible for yer own horse." He paused, and notwithstanding his new shirt and bolo tie, spat into the dirt. "They're all saddled and ready to go, but some of 'em tend to blow out, so before you get aboard, check that cinch. Everybody know how to do that?"

A chorus of confirming shouts made Chase grin and shake his head. These dudes would sooner die than admit they didn't know their way around horses. He could identify. Six weeks ago he'd been the same way. He made a mental note to check Amanda's cinch, although she might be the one greenhorn who would know how. She'd had her own horse, after all. Probably was also given a sports car when she was sixteen and had tuition paid to a fancy college. He needed to remember all that when he was spinning fantasies involving Amanda.

"Now, as soon as Eb Whitlock shows up, we'll start on out to the homestead," Duane said.

Chase realized then that Eb's big palomino wasn't tied up to the hitching post, and Eb wasn't part of the crowd of men clustered around Ry. He could guess how steamed Ry must be, considering he didn't want Eb to be part of the wedding in the first place.

"Here he comes!" shouted someone as Eb's dual-wheeled pickup and horse trailer rumbled down the road sending up clouds of dust. Eb braked to a stop and the dust cloud settled over the wedding party and the horses Duane and Curtis had so carefully groomed for the event. Men brushed at their shoulders, women at their skirts as Eb, wearing a pearl gray western coat, vest and matching hat, climbed down from the air-conditioned cab of his truck with a politician's wave and his truck-grille smile.

"Howdy, folks," he said. "Nice day for a wedding, ain't it? Hey, Duane, give me a hand unloading Gold Strike," he called as he started back toward the trailer.

"Shore." As Duane passed Chase in the buggy, he paused. "Guess you and Leigh might as well get the rest of 'em mounted up while I help unload the wonder horse," he said in a low tone.

"He knew better than to ask me," Leigh grumbled as she came up beside the buggy. "You just watch. That gelding will be covered with horse jewelry."

Chase laughed. "What?"

"Silver on every inch of leather except the seat of the saddle. Just wait and see. In the meantime, we'd better divvy up these ponies. Give Amanda Pussywillow."

Chase climbed down from the buggy. "I thought Ry's stepmother wanted her."

"She did, but she doesn't ride as well as Amanda."

"How do you know how well Amanda rides?"

"I was out in the yard holding my stomach and watching for the ambulance when she tore in here yesterday." Leigh looked up at Chase from under her pink maid-of-honor Stetson. "She has the makings of a cowgirl, you know."

"Yeah, right. I'm sure she'd give up her big paycheck in New York to come out and wrangle for the True Love."

"You never know until you ask."

Chase's stomach flip-flopped at the idea and he changed the subject. "Okay, Ry's best man will be on Mikey, right?"

"Right. He wanted Destiny, but forget that. He thinks he's a hotshot around horses, but he doesn't have a clue."

"What's his name again?"

"Stewart. Stewart Hepplewaite. Now let's see." Leigh tapped her finger against her chin. "We'll put Ry's stepmother on Bobby. He's steady. And Ry's mother on Billy."

Chase forced himself to concentrate as she rattled off the rest of the horse assignments he was supposed to handle. He started toward the group of people on the lawn just as a collective gasp made him turn around to see what they were all staring at. He was nearly blinded by the reflected light coming off Gold Strike's saddle, headstall and breastplate as the big horse backed out of the trailer. But Leigh hadn't been entirely right about the horse jewelry. The trim on the leather wasn't silver. It was gold.

Chase chuckled and continued with his duties. As he was approaching Stewart Hepplewaite to give him the bad news that he'd be riding Mikey and not Destiny, Ry caught his arm.

"Did you see that s.o.b.?" he muttered.

"Meaning Whitlock," Chase said, holding back a smile.

"He's trying to impress Freddy, and convince her she's making a mistake marrying me instead of him."

Chase couldn't resist. "Think it's working?"

Ry scowled. "Oh, hell, of course not, but the guy's so damned irritating." Ry lowered his voice. "I'd love to nail him for these ranch accidents, just for the pure satisfaction of it."

"Just don't let the fact that he's a jerk get in the way of clear thinking, buddy. I hope it's him instead of somebody close, like Duane or Belinda. But that's not always the way things work." He clapped Ry on the shoulder. "Time to mount up, bridegroom. Red Devil looks almost as antsy as you do, so be careful. We'd all hate to see you land on your butt during the ceremony."

"If it happens, I'm blaming Whitlock. Between that gold tack and the shine on his teeth, he could signal passing aircraft. I'll be amazed if he doesn't spook somebody's horse."

"Hey, you two, get a move on," Leigh called over to them.

Ry glanced at Chase. "Okay, I'm going."

"You could look a little happier about it," Chase called after him. Then he went in search of Stewart Hepplewaite.

Twenty minutes later, the procession jingled and clopped down the road toward the homestead. The wedding would be late. Ry and Freddy led the way, so they wouldn't get too much dust on their wedding clothes. Leigh and Duane had set up the procession like a cattle drive, with each of them riding point. Curtis and Ernie manned the middle as swing riders, Davis and Rusty rode flank and Chase rode drag with Jack, behind the buggy. Belinda handled Clyde, the ranch's big draft horse, with ease. Between her and Dexter sat Chloe, whose tongue was hanging out, ears alert. Propped behind the seat was an easel and the framed lintel from the old homestead.

Chase had asked to be in the back, because he thought it was the safest place for Bart, who was laced into the cradleboard on his back.

Ahead of him Amanda rode next to Stewart Hepplewaite and the two of them were laughing and talking like old friends. Stewart was her kind of guy, no doubt, a polished New Yorker who could probably name every damn tune that had played on the radio the night before. Chase felt like strangling Stewart Hepplewaite.

Miraculously, the procession arrived without incident at the clearing where the homestead had once stood.

Duane dismounted and set up the easel with the framed
lintel propped on it. Positioning his horse beside the easel, the minister turned to face the group while Ry and
Stewart Hepplewaite arranged their mounts on his left
and Leigh guided her horse to the minister's right. The
horses snorted and stamped some, but none of them
acted up except Red Devil, Ry's big chestnut. He kept
throwing his head back, and Chase wondered how long
it would be before Ry caught it on the chin.

Freddy and Eb Whitlock moved to the back of the
group, which assembled on either side of the clearing.
Now that Hepplewaite was otherwise occupied, Chase
maneuvered next to Amanda. Curtis untied his guitar
from his saddle and began to play the wedding march as
Freddy laid her hand on Eb's arm and they nudged their
horses into a rhythmic walk.

Chase hadn't expected the ceremony to get to him, but
his eyes began to burn and his throat closed up. He
glanced at Amanda and discovered she was looking
straight at him, her eyes shining with unshed tears. He
felt as if he'd been kicked in the gut by Gold Strike.
Caught in the brightness of her blue eyes, he couldn't
look away as Curtis played the final note on the guitar
and Freddy and Ry began exchanging their vows.

Chase had attended a few weddings, mostly for
truckers he knew. He'd always thought the language was
ridiculous. Everyone knew people didn't stay married
"until death do us part" anymore.

And yet . . .

This time, looking into Amanda's eyes, the words took
on a luster he'd never heard. Maybe it was because he
knew Freddy and Ry would make it. They had love and
grit enough to last until death took them. And if one
couple could make it . . .

Amanda's gaze softened, and Chase would have bet money she was thinking the same thing. Then she smiled, and that smile sent sunshine pouring into his aching heart. Maybe, just maybe . . .

A ripple of laughter from the group brought his attention back to the ceremony. He blinked, not realizing at first what had happened. Then he remembered Duane's instructions about tightening cinches. Apparently, Stewart Hepplewaite hadn't followed orders. As he'd leaned toward Ry to hand him the ring, his saddle had begun to rotate.

Everyone stared in mesmerized silence as Stewart clutched the horn and rode the saddle slowly down. Gravity pulled it toward the underbelly of the horse, which is where he would have ended up if Ry hadn't reined Red Devil in closer at the last minute, stopping the fall when Stewart was perpendicular to the ground.

Stewart landed with his head in Ry's lap.

13

THE LOOSE CINCH ended the run of good luck. Red Devil tossed his head back for the hundredth time, but Ry's attention was on Stewart reclining in his lap and Red Devil knocked Ry's hat off. The hat spinning to the ground spooked Maureen, Freddy's mare, who reared, her hooves coming down on the easel holding the framed lintel.

Both Ry's mother and stepmother started screaming. That noise, added to the splintering of the easel, sent the minister's horse into a bucking fit that dislodged the minister, who slid from the horse's rump onto a small but very thorny hedgehog cactus. Chloe leapt from the buggy, her usual restraint destroyed, and raced around barking. Eb Whitlock spun in ineffectual circles on Gold Strike, seemingly unable to control the horse as sunlight flashed off the gold tack until Chase saw spots in front of his eyes.

Chase backed his horse away from the general pandemonium, not wanting to endanger Bart. But Amanda waded right in on Pussywillow. Chase watched in open admiration as she grabbed Gold Strike's bridle and halted the palomino's spin. Chloe miraculously obeyed Amanda's command to return to the buggy, and then Amanda worked side by side with the cowhands soothing mounts and reassuring edgy riders.

Eventually, Stewart was sitting upright on Mikey once more, the ring was placed on Freddy's finger, and the minister, who chose to stand, pronounced them husband and wife. They kissed as passionately as their restless mounts would allow, and Curtis played a recessional as they straggled back to the ranch house, the minister riding high in his stirrups for the duration of the trip.

By the time they returned, the clearing around the ranch house looked like a used-truck lot. Ranching friends from all over the valley had arrived for the reception, and they crowded around to congratulate the bride and groom. Chase reined his horse past the well-wishers and headed for the hitching post. Bart was beginning to fuss.

As Chase dismounted, Amanda rode up on Pussywillow. "I'll take him now," she said, swinging down and tethering Pussywillow.

Chase eased the leather straps off his shoulders as she stood behind him to take the cradleboard. "Got him?"

"Yes."

"I think he's getting hungry." Chase turned. "If you'll hold him, I'll unlace this thing. I don't think you want to try and carry him through that mob still strapped in."

"Probably not." Amanda held the board steady while Chase pulled the laces free. "He was good though, during the ceremony. I was afraid he'd cry and spoil it."

Chase laughed as he pulled Bart from the wrapped blanket. "And goodness knows, we wouldn't have wanted to spoil the ceremony. It was so picture perfect."

Amanda chuckled. "Can you believe the way Stewart slid around into Ry's lap? What an idiot."

"I don't think he tightened his cinch, do you?" Chase said with a grin as he hoisted Bart to his shoulder. Life was turning out pretty well, after all.

"Nope." Amanda's eyes brimmed with merriment. "I wouldn't have missed that wedding for the world. What a hoot."

"Sure was." He couldn't stop gazing into her eyes. "You did a great job settling people down. Leigh must be right. She predicted that you'd make a good cowgirl."

"Did she?" Amanda looked pleased, and his hopes soared higher. "Coming from Leigh, that's a big compliment."

He hesitated. "Amanda, we need to talk. I—"

Bartholomew's cry interrupted him.

"We'll talk," Amanda said. "Later."

"Is that a promise?"

"Yes." She held out the cradleboard. "Trade you."

He held Bart in one arm and took the cradleboard with his free hand. "I'll be waiting."

"Me, too." Then with a smile that turned his insides to mush, she took the baby from him and left.

AMANDA KEPT EXPECTING the wedding reception to wind down, but the party seemed to gain momentum as afternoon turned into evening. Freddy and Ry showed no signs of leaving on their honeymoon—a week in the pine forests of Mount Lemmon, little more than an hour's drive away. The guests obviously felt that as long as the bride and groom remained, the party should continue in full swing.

Amanda surveyed the patio, proud of the way everything looked and her part in making it that way. While strolling *mariachis* played, people ignored the heat, drank beer and margaritas and ate Belinda's food as if no one even considered the possibility of food poisoning. Yet Amanda couldn't help wondering if they would be so unconcerned once they'd heard the gossip that would inevitably spring up surrounding yesterday's disaster. A rumor of food poisoning in one New York restaurant had damaged its reputation beyond what any of her ad campaigns had been able to repair. She didn't want that happening to the True Love. She had to admit her growing fondness for the place, or maybe it was the tall cowboy who was one-third owner she was growing fond of.

Bartholomew seemed to enjoy the color and activity of the party. She alternated between putting him in his carrier, where he sometimes dozed off, and holding him. She slipped into Freddy's office twice to feed him, but otherwise she kept him in the thick of things. He acted like a magnet for the guests, and nearly everyone came by to admire and coo. Everybody except Chase, that is. But that was okay. The promise of talking to him before the day ended shone like a beacon for Amanda. She hadn't been mistaken. The wedding ceremony had stirred him as much as it had her. Whatever misunderstanding had caused him to stomp off this morning would be ironed out.

Not that the problems would end there. She'd decided to tell her family about Chase, but she didn't expect them to react well. And the logistics of a future relationship would be tricky, unless Chase agreed to the plan she'd dreamed up this afternoon. She could hardly wait to tell him about it. And then there was the medallion. She'd finally figured out where she'd seen one like it.

Duane came by her table, a beer in one hand and an empty coffee can in the other. "Havin' fun?"

"Yes, I am," she said with a smile.

"Jest wanted to thank you for helpin' with the commotion out there." He angled his head in the direction of the road to the old homestead. "Didn't know you was so handy with horses."

"I'm glad I could help."

"You recall how Red Devil was tossin' his head?"

Amanda nodded. "He's pretty high-spirited."

"Not that high. When we took off his bridle, we found a big old burr under there. Must've been drivin' him crazy."

"That was unlucky."

"More'n unlucky." Duane scowled and spat a stream of tobacco into the coffee can. "That don't happen 'round here. The hands are real careful about stuff like that." Duane eyed her. "I think some low-down snake put it under there on purpose."

"You mean as a wedding prank?"

"Maybe more'n a prank." He gave her a dark look. "Did Chase tell you about what's been goin' on?"

"No." She grew uneasy. "I don't know what you're talking about."

Duane nodded and glanced away. "Guess he didn't want to worry you none."

Alarm ran through her and she thought immediately of the snake under her bed. "So what is going on?"

"I'd best let Chase tell you." Duane reached out and wiggled Bartholomew's foot. "See you later, cowpoke."

"Duane—" She closed her mouth as he walked away resolutely. Now she had a second reason to talk to Chase. If this place was booby-trapped, she wanted to know it. She had a child to protect.

CHASE LOVED HIS SON, but the more he thought about this critical talk with Amanda, the more he wanted to have it without the distraction of a baby. He studied the situation in the patio and finally approached Belinda, tossing his empty beer can into a bin of recyclables on his way.

She glanced up with a twinkle in her eye. "I hope all the festivities are giving you ideas, Chase."

He grinned at her. "Could be, Belinda. Matter of fact, I'm here to ask a favor. I need to talk to Amanda alone, and I wondered if you'd watch Bart for a little while. Last time I checked, he was sound asleep, so I don't think he'll be much trouble."

"That little baby would never be too much trouble. Dexter's been wanting to see him. I'll take Bartholomew over and sit with Dexter and Chloe for a while."

"That's only if it's okay with Amanda. I haven't asked her yet."

Belinda smiled, and for a moment she looked like a young girl again. "You leave her to me. I'll set it up. Where would you like her to meet you?"

Chase sorted through the possibilities. Guests clustered everywhere—the patio, the main room of the house and the front porch. "Out in back, I guess, just beyond the gate. I'll wait for her," he said.

"How romantic. I'll send her out to you." Belinda turned and headed for the table where Amanda sat talking to Ry's mother.

Chase mentally crossed his fingers and strode toward the back-patio gate. On the way he tried to figure out what to say to her. The word *love* buzzed around in his brain like a honeybee. He wasn't sure he was ready for that word yet, but he was ready to tell Amanda that she meant a lot to him and that he didn't want to lose her. He wondered if he'd have the nerve to ask her to stay in Arizona. Leigh thought he should. Maybe there was work in her field in Tucson. She'd seemed pleased about being called a cowgirl. She got along with everybody. Maybe she was beginning to like it here, and if not, he'd make love to her so often, she wouldn't have time to think about where she was living.

He glanced up at the sky as he slipped through the gate, leaving it open a couple of feet. A few clouds remained clustered around the mountains, and once in a while they'd light up as if somebody had turned on a switch inside them. But it didn't look as if it would rain tonight, after all. Selfishly, Chase was glad. It gave him this chance to be outside in the warm summer night, waiting for Amanda. He moved into the shadows near the thick adobe wall. The laughter and music from the reception breached the wall, but the adobe buffered the noise just enough so that he and Amanda would be able to talk.

The trouble was, when she opened the gate and stepped through, with moonlight gilding her hair as she glanced around for him, he no longer wanted to talk. "Over here," he said, his voice stretched as tight as the fabric of his jeans. He stepped from the shadows and she came toward him, moving quickly.

When she was within reach, he pulled her close with a groan, his mouth seeking hers. He thought his chest would explode when he realized she was grabbing at him with an equal hunger, her fingers digging into his back, her pelvis pushing hard against his erection.

He kissed her mouth, her cheeks, the curve of her throat. "I need you, Amanda."

"I need you, too," she whispered desperately. "Why did you get so angry with me this morning?"

"It was stupid." He leaned down and kissed the swell of her breasts above the scooped neckline of her dress. "When you told me how good I was, I thought you only wanted me for sex, like every other woman I've ever taken to bed."

"Oh, Chase." There was amusement in her voice as she stroked his hair. "You thought I considered you a sex object?"

"Something like that." He unfastened the top two buttons of her dress and slipped his hand beneath her bra.

"And you wanted me to think of you as more than that."

"Yes. I—" As he stroked her warm breast heavy with milk, he lost his train of thought and picked up a new one. "Ah, Amanda, you feel like silk. Let's forget about the reception. I'll get Bart and we can head back to the cottage."

She arched against his palm. "What if I feel like a sex object?"

"It's not like that, and you know it."

"I do?" she said softly.

His hand stilled and he gazed into her eyes. "I don't know if I can be any good at this, but I . . . want to work something out. I want to be with you . . . somehow."

"That's an interesting thought." Her lips curved. "Half-formed, but interesting."

"I'm glad you think so." He massaged her breast and leaned down to nibble at the corner of her mouth. "Now let's go get Bart and head for the cottage so we can work out the details."

"You know if we do that we won't work out any details, and we have so much to talk about, so much we don't know about each other." She slipped her fingers under the chain around his neck. "Like this. Where did you get it?"

He lifted his head to gaze down at her. "Not from some other lover, if that's what you're worried about."

"Considering your independent nature, I didn't think so, either. Did the medallion belong to your mother?"

He released her and stepped back, suddenly wary. "Why?"

"Because if it did, I might know where it came from. My mother has one just like it. It was a citizenship award in eighth grade from a school in Brooklyn. She told me once that there's also a plaque at the school with the name of everyone who's ever won that award."

His chest tightened. When he was younger, he'd wondered what the little medallion meant and why his mother's name was inscribed on the back, but as he'd grown older, he'd just accepted it as the only part of her he had left. At fifteen, he'd bought a chain for it and he'd become so used to feeling its weight around his neck, he'd forgotten it was there.

When he started to speak, he realized his throat had seized up on him. He cleared it and tried again. "I . . . I guess that would be nice to know. Where it came from, I mean."

She grabbed his arm. "It could mean more than that. Maybe that school is a place to start, a way to find her."

He glanced away from the excitement in her expression. "Maybe. I know you want the information for Bart's sake, but I—"

"I want it for your sake."

That got his attention. "Me? Why me?"

"Chase, you didn't come from nowhere. You have grandparents, great-grandparents, aunts, uncles and cousins. You have family. Everyone does. Some good, some bad. One of my great-grandfathers was a horse thief. So what? That doesn't mean I'm a horse thief. The point is, you have connections. We should find them."

He drew her slowly back into his arms. "We?"

"I want to help."

"You might not like what you find."

"You weren't listening. You're not responsible for what's in your family tree. But wouldn't it be nice to know you had one?"

The concept was a little mind-boggling, and he was pretty sure if they located his mother it wouldn't be a pretty sight, but she looked so happy about the prospect of digging into his background he decided to go along with it. "Sure. Sure it would." He leaned closer, needing her lips against his. "Now, let's—"

"Wait. I have to ask you something else."

"Remind me never to give you a whole day to think about things."

She looked up at him earnestly. "Is there a problem here at the True Love?"

"Yes. Too damn many activities, when all I want to do is this." His mouth descended again.

She leaned away from his kiss. "I'm serious. Duane hinted at some trouble but he said you should be the one to tell me."

Thanks, Duane. Great timing. He sighed. Then he cupped her face in his hands and gazed down at her. "I don't know if there's trouble or not. We've had some incidents."

Anxiety shone in her eyes. "Like what?" she asked.

"Most of it's the sort of thing you could expect around a ranch. Stock tank leaks, breaks in the fence, gates left open. But the morning you got here, somebody contaminated the water in the horse troughs. Thank God we discovered it before any horses got sick. And then there was the food poisoning. Ry doesn't think that was an accident, either."

Amanda's eyes were wide. "Duane found a burr under Red Devil's bridle when he turned him into the corral. Duane thinks it was put there on purpose, to louse up the wedding."

"Or maybe one of the hands screwed up," Chase said.

"What about the snake?"

"Oh, I don't think—"

"Why not? If someone wants to ruin the True Love's reputation or bring down the property's value, all of that makes sense. Would anyone have reason to want the True Love to go under?"

Chase released her again and rubbed the back of his neck. A headache was lodging at the base of his skull. That indicated tension, which could bring on a back spasm. And the way the party was going, he wouldn't be swimming laps tonight. "The three of us, Ry, me and Joe Gilardini, the cop, bought this place as an investment, figuring to sell it in a couple of years to developers."

Amanda drew in a sharp breath. "Do Freddy and Leigh know that? Does Belinda?"

Chase nodded. "Nobody liked the idea when they heard it. There's a steady campaign to get each of us to change our mind and become a gentleman rancher, instead. But Ry thinks somebody is going beyond that to outright sabotage. If the ranch isn't worth much, we might sell just to get out from under. Then someone else, someone who wants to keep it as a ranch, could buy it."

Amanda shivered. "If someone could be hurt, or worse, I say let them have the ranch, whoever they are, if they're that desperate."

Chase was amazed at how he rebelled at that idea. "In the first place, we don't know who's doing it, and in the second place, speaking for Ry and me, we're not about to give up the True Love that easy."

"I thought you planned to sell it to developers eventually, anyway."

Chase massaged his neck and chuckled, mostly at himself. "Yeah, that's the way it was supposed to work."

"You don't want to sell, do you?"

It was an interesting question, and Chase didn't have the answer yet. "I guess that depends. There's a little more to the decision now than there was a few days ago. When I think of you and Bart, I have to consider the money angle. As a guest ranch, the True Love hasn't ever made a lot of money."

She cocked her head and gazed at him. "Then I guess this is the perfect time to tell you my idea. It finally hit me that cowboys are all the rage right now. If you come back to New York with me, I could set up modeling agency interviews. I know this business, Chase, and with that cowboy look you've developed, you'd be making more money than you ever dreamed of in no time at all." She paused. "And we could be together, which is something you said you wanted."

He stared at her and wondered if maybe he'd misunderstood. "This isn't a cowboy look, Amanda. This is what I am, now. It's what I was meant to be, I think, even when I was driving truck."

"Exactly! So you're authentic, and that would shine through in the ads. You'd be a huge success, Chase. I've been watching the way you move, and you'd be a natural in front of the camera. I don't know why I didn't think of it sooner."

He couldn't believe that such a warm, sexy woman could come up with such a harebrained idea. Rounding up members of his family tree he could go along with, but parading around in front of a camera pretending to be a cowboy instead of being out here on the ranch actually living that life would be the worst kind of hell he could imagine. Couldn't she see that? "It's not for me, Amanda."

She looked as if he'd slapped her. "You're rejecting the idea just like that? Without thinking about it?"

"Doesn't take much time to think about an idea like that. I'd hate it."

She spoke slowly, carefully. "Then what did you think we would do?"

And he saw it all very clearly, then. She'd come up with that plan because it would allow her to stay in her world and make him an acceptable part of it, in the bargain. He wouldn't be a trucker or a cowboy tied to some ranch in the middle of nowhere, he'd be a celebrity model. A prize. He shook his head. "God knows, Amanda. Certainly not anything like that."

"Then what?" she persisted. "Both of us stay here and watch this ranch go down the tubes? From what you've said, this is a very risky venture, with saboteurs lurking in the wings. Is that what you want for yourself? For me and your son?"

She made it sound pretty foolish, when she put it like that. But he couldn't change his basic nature to make her happy. And apparently she couldn't change hers. "No, I wouldn't want that for you or Bart," he said quietly. "But I'm willing to take the risk for myself. So I guess that about takes care of our talk, Amanda. If you'll just promise to bring Bart out West once in a while, so I can see him—" Chase's throat closed and he couldn't go on. The thought of Amanda and Bart leaving hurt too bad to think about, but they would leave.

"Dammit, Chase, is that really all you have to say?"

He looked away from the tears in her eyes. "Guess so." From the corner of his eye he could see her rebuttoning her dress with trembling fingers. Then she straightened her shoulders and lifted her chin. She had guts. He'd give her that.

"I'll make plane reservations for tomorrow. I'm sure Duane will be taking a load of people out to the airport, anyway, so I'll just ride along."

He didn't say anything. He was afraid if he opened his mouth, he might start begging, which wouldn't do any good, anyway. She didn't want the life he had to offer, so he might as well save himself the humiliation.

Leigh stuck her head around the partially open gate. "Hey, you two lovebirds! Freddy and Ry are finally leaving for Mount Lemmon. Get in here and help us pelt them with rice!" Then she disappeared.

Chase looked at Amanda. He hadn't known he could hurt this bad. "I owe them a good sendoff," he said, his voice cracking. "But you don't have to do this if you don't want to."

"I want to," she said, and whirled away to stride purposefully through the gate.

Chase had never seen her look more beautiful.

AMANDA COULDN'T BOOK a flight out of Tucson until midafternoon the next day. Afraid she would start screaming if she had to hang around the ranch all morning being pleasant, she decided to go somewhere more private. She called the bunkhouse and asked the cowboy who answered to saddle Pussywillow for her.

"Is Chase going with you?" said the hand, who sounded like Curtis.

She realized she'd never get away if she didn't lie. "No, but I'm only going down to the main road and back. I don't need Chase for that."

"Okay. I'll bring her up for you."

Amanda laced Bartholomew tightly into the cradleboard and lifted it onto her shoulders. It was heavier than she'd expected, but she figured she could manage. She thought of making up some excuse to take the cellular phone, but that would arouse suspicion. A ride to the mailbox and back hardly required a phone connection. As she started down the flagstone path leading away from the house, she saw Curtis riding up the road, leading Pussywillow. So far, so good.

"Where you goin'?" asked a deep male voice.

She turned to see Dexter sitting on the porch, Chloe by his side.

She tried to sound casual. "For a little ride."

"No one? By—alone?"

"Nope." She smiled. "Bartholomew's going, too."

"You need Chase."

No, she didn't. Not anymore. Not ever again. "I'll manage just fine, Dexter."

"Take the dog."

Amanda considered that for a moment and rejected the idea. A dog on the trail might be more trouble than she was worth if she spent time chasing rabbits and gophers. "I'm really not going that far," she said, gritting her teeth to keep from shouting her impatience to be off. She glanced back toward the road. "Well, here's Curtis with Pussywillow. See you later, Dexter."

She hurried down the walk and out the gate to the hitching post where Curtis had dismounted and was holding his horse and Pussywillow by the reins.

He looked doubtfully at the cradleboard. "Didn't know you were takin' the baby."

"He's very light," she fibbed. These Western men were a little too overprotective for her taste.

"I should probably go with you." He glanced uncertainly around the yard. "Where's Chase?"

"I don't know for sure." She smiled her brightest smile. "He partied pretty hard last night."

Curtis nodded. "Like the rest of us. My head feels like a barrel cactus this mornin'."

"I didn't want to bother him, but I longed for another ride on Pussywillow. She has such a nice gait."

"She's a good one, all right." He studied her. "And I've seen you sit a horse. You know what you're doin'. Guess it's all right." He grinned. "Besides, if I rode with you, I'd probably get into trouble with Chase."

Not anymore, Amanda thought. "I really don't need an escort," she said. "But thanks for being concerned."

"I'll help you up, at least."

She accepted the two cupped hands he offered and placed her booted foot in them. The cradleboard threw her off-balance just enough to make mounting from ground level difficult. She'd have to find a fallen log when she remounted. She settled herself in the saddle and smiled down at Curtis. "Thanks."

"As long as you don't get off again until you get back, you'll be fine." He adjusted his hat. "Guess I'll go in and trouble Belinda for a cup of coffee. Maybe I'll still be here when you get back. That way I can help you down again."

"Maybe." She reined Pussywillow around. "Thanks again," she called over her shoulder as she started down the lane at a slow walk so she wouldn't jostle Bartholomew.

CHASE TOOK a cup of coffee out to the patio and squinted up at the sun. Must be damn near eleven in the morning. He rubbed a hand over his bristled chin. He felt as if somebody had hit him over the head with a tire iron. Switching from beer to margaritas after Freddy and Ry left might not have been such a great idea, but it had kept tension from attacking his back muscles. He remembered dancing with Rosa, who was old enough to be his mother, and smashing the hell out of a *piñata*. He even remembered asking Curtis to saddle up Gutbuster, the True Love's most dangerous bronc. Curtis had refused, thank God.

Some perverse impulse drew him out the back patio gate to the scene of the crime. Funny, but the spot where his whole future had collapsed didn't look much different from the rest of the surrounding desert. He glanced up the trail in the direction of the cottage and wondered if she was in there packing. Or hiding.

A cloud eased over the sun and the wind picked up. Maybe today the rain would start, but Belinda had told him they'd probably get a lot of wind, first. She'd also told him to go back to his room and shave, but he didn't much feel like it. Duane was the one driving to the airport, not him. And he was one of the owners of the place, wasn't he? An owner should be able to walk around unshaven without the cook chewing his behind about it. Belinda was just ticked because Amanda and the baby were leaving. Maybe Belinda even thought he could do something about that, but the time was long past.

The wind almost took his hat, and he pulled it lower over his eyes. He gazed out over the desert, where a couple of dust devils whirled across the desert floor like columns of smoke. Then he picked out a third, a bigger one, looking more gray than tan. He narrowed his eyes. Wait a minute. That wasn't a dust devil.

He dashed his coffee in the dirt and sprinted back into the patio. Wrenching open the French doors, he bellowed out Leigh's name.

"In here!" she called from Freddy's office. "And keep your voice down, cowboy. Some of us have headaches from last night, you know."

He covered the distance to the office door in three quick strides. "There's a fire," he said, breathing hard. "Looks like it's near the mouth of Rogue Canyon."

14

LEIGH JUMPED from the desk chair uttering a very unladylike oath. "You're sure? It's not just a dust devil?"

"I'm sure."

Leigh swore again and punched in the Rural-Metro Fire Department's number on the telephone. After consulting with the dispatcher, she hung up and called the bunkhouse. "We've got a fire up at the mouth of Rogue Canyon," she said. "Rural-Metro's going to see if they can line up some choppers with buckets. Have Curtis, Rusty and Jack start hosing down the corrals. The rest of you get shovels and mount up." She replaced the receiver and glanced at Chase. "Could you tell which way the wind was blowing?"

"East, I'd say."

"So unless the wind shifts, the ranch won't be in danger, but an easterly wind could blow that sucker up the canyon, right toward our summer pasture and our herd. Ever fought a brushfire before?"

"Nope." He relished the challenge of protecting the True Love. As a bonus, fighting the fire would take his mind off Amanda.

"Go get on your oldest clothes and meet me back here in five minutes." Leigh grimaced. "I hate to do this, but I'm calling Ry and Freddy on Mount Lemmon. They'd want to be here. Happy honeymoon."

"Yeah." Chase started to say something about the True Love Curse, but the ringing telephone stopped him.

Leigh grabbed it. "Yeah? Just a minute. I'll check." She covered the mouthpiece with one hand. "Curtis wants to know if Amanda and the baby are back from their ride yet."

Fear whacked him in the chest. "Their what?"

"Ride. You didn't know about it?"

"No, I didn't know about it. Let me talk to him." Chase crossed to the desk and took the receiver from Leigh. "What's this about a ride?"

"She said it would be a short one, Chase. But that was almost three hours ago." Curtis sounded scared. "Took the baby in that cradleboard. I thought about tagging along, but I thought you'd get mad."

Chase didn't want to waste time debating that issue. "I'll find her." He pressed the disconnect button and dialed the cottage. No answer. He dumped the receiver into the cradle. "Let me check out front. Maybe she's just coming in or something," he said to Leigh before dashing toward the front porch.

He willed her to be riding down the lane as he flung open the front door. She wasn't. He stepped out on the porch and strained to see down the dusty road. No Amanda. The little bit of coffee he'd drunk tasted like acid on his tongue.

"Went that way," Dexter said.

Chase whirled and glanced at the old cowboy sitting in his cane chair, Chloe at his feet. "Which way, Dexter?"

"That way." Dexter jerked his thumb over his right shoulder in the direction of Rogue Canyon.

Chase tried to calm his rolling stomach and deny what he knew in his bones to be true. "How do you know? You can't see the fork in the road from here."

Dexter gestured toward his walker. "I visited... no... followed her. She went slow."

Leigh came out on the porch, her truck keys in one hand and Ry's cellular phone in the other. "No sign of her?"

Chase felt his chest tightening, his back threatening to spasm. He couldn't allow that now. "I think she might be up in Rogue Canyon," he said quietly.

"Oh, God. The fire."

Dexter clutched her sleeve. "Fire?"

"There's a fire at the mouth of Rogue Canyon, Dex," she said. She laid a hand on Chase's arm. "Maybe she's on her way back."

"Maybe." He spoke in a monotone, afraid any emotion might start a reaction inside that would leave him screaming with the terror he felt at the possibility that Amanda and Bart were trapped in the canyon by the fire.

"Forget changing clothes," Leigh said. "We can always get new clothes. We'll just go to the stables. I'll bet she'll be there when we arrive."

"Yeah. Let's go." Chase jogged to the truck, his gut filled with tension.

Leigh was right behind him. They both piled in and she started the truck. The back tires spit dirt and gravel as she peeled out. "I'm sure she's out of there by now, Chase."

"And I think you're trying your damnedest to deny what we both know. Be honest with me, Leigh. You're supposed to have these psychic powers. Where is she?"

Leigh wouldn't answer him, which was as good as an answer.

He slammed the door panel with his fist. "What did she have to go off like that for, with the baby? Talk about stupid!"

"You drank yourself silly last night and she took a ride this morning. We all handle stress differently, Chase. She's a good rider. It wouldn't have been risky except for this fire."

He was desperate for someone or something to blame. "But I told her the desert was dry as a bone! Why didn't it rain yesterday, Leigh? Where is the damn rain?"

"You'll get her back, Chase."

Chase's throat felt as if he'd swallowed road tar. "I have to. I couldn't live if she . . ." He couldn't finish the sentence.

Leigh shot him a look. "Does she know that?"

"No." He stared sightlessly down the road. "Because I didn't know. Until now."

Leigh took a curve fast enough to throw him against the door. "Then make this fire count for something," she said.

Moments later they arrived at the corrals and Chase scanned the busy area. There were lots of people, lots of horses. No Amanda. He clenched his teeth. He knew what he had to do.

As he got out of the truck, Chloe jumped from the back and ran up to him. "Hey," he called after Leigh as she headed for the hitching post. "What's Chloe doing here?"

Leigh didn't pause. "Dexter sent her along," she said over her shoulder. "Didn't you hear him tell her to come with us?"

In three long strides he'd caught up with her. "No, and I think she'll only be in the way."

"You have to understand what this is like for Dexter. His range is burning and he can't do anything but sit and wait for the news. He did the only thing he could. He sent Chloe." Leigh glanced at him. "I'd advise you to take her with you when you ride up into the canyon."

He stared at her. "You won't try to stop me from going?"

"No. If Amanda's smart, she's waiting up by the pond. A helicopter can't land there. But if somebody goes up on Mikey, they can bring her down. We got Mikey from the forest service and he's old, but he's fire-trained. Pussywillow isn't, but she likes Chloe. Chloe may be able to settle her down. It's worth a shot."

"Thanks, Leigh. I thought I'd get an argument because of my back."

She smiled gently. "I know you have to go. Remember the deep breathing to keep your back relaxed. Take two blankets from the bunkhouse and soak them in the horse trough before you leave." Her brown eyes glowed with encouragement. "You'll make it."

Fifteen minutes later, Chase held on to Leigh's confidence like a talisman as he started along the trail at a brisk trot, the wet blankets tied to the back of his saddle dripping water down Mikey's flanks. His shirt and jeans were already starting to dry, and the blankets would dry out quickly, so he had to get there before that happened. He loped the horse when he could, always aware of Chloe racing by his side. Fortunately, she was in good shape. He carried extra canteens of water, and he'd douse her with them when they reached the fire line.

With the wind blowing away from him, he didn't smell it until he was close to the billowing brown smoke, but he could hear it crackling, popping and hissing as water stored inside the saguaros and barrels began to boil. Mikey twitched his ears and danced nervously, but he kept going.

Then Chase saw the fire ahead of him on the trail, the flames licking through the sage and creosote, leaving glowing twigs as it passed. The heat rolled toward him, but the fire moved away, carried by the wind upward toward the canyon. Toward Amanda and Bart. He had to outrun it.

Mikey nickered and tossed his head when the flames came into view. And he's the fire-trained horse, Chase thought, dismounting and calling Chloe over to douse her with water. He gave Chloe a drink from his cupped hands before he poured the contents of the canteen over her black-and-white fur. "Stay close, now," he said, mounting up and untying one of the blankets to wrap around his shoulders.

He poured another canteen over Mikey, concentrating on the animal's mane and tail. Then he pulled the still-damp blanket around his shoulders. The smell of wet wool, wet horse and wet dog mingled with the sharp bite of charred desert as he started picking his way around the ragged edges of the fire, working his way to the head of it. Adrenaline pumped through him, sharpening his senses and delaying fear. He had to get through and he had to come back with Amanda and Bart. He had no choice.

Mikey pulled at the bit and shied whenever a small creature bounded past them in panicked retreat. A slithering rattlesnake momentarily distracted Chloe, who stopped to growl and raise her hackles. But the snake slipped out of sight before Chloe could get very excited. None of the creatures seemed to care much about a dog and a man on a horse. Survival hung in the balance as they raced from the flames.

At last Chase made it back to the main trail, just yards from the entrance to the canyon. He was ahead of the blaze now, and smoke billowed around him, making him cough and choke. Through watering eyes he tried to gauge the distance the fire had to travel before it blocked the canyon entrance. As he saw how quickly the escape route could be closed, even adrenaline couldn't prevent the cold sweat of fear.

Whipping off the blanket and holding it under one arm, he concentrated all his energies on getting Mikey up the trail as quickly as possible. Canyon walls that had seemed so sheltering now closed in like a prison. Except for the crackling behind him, the air was hushed. No birds sang, no insects buzzed—they'd already evacuated the area.

He rose above the level of the smoke, took a deep lungful of clean air and glanced at Chloe scrambling up the trail ahead of him. "Find Amanda!" he called, and Chloe's answering bark was a reassuring sound in the stillness. She bounded up the trail, slipping on loose shale but always regaining her balance and hurtling on. Soon she was out of sight.

AMANDA WONDERED if she'd imagined the bark as she sat on a rock next to the pond and cuddled Bartholomew. She'd tried not to convey her fear, but he'd picked it up and was wailing pitifully. Pussywillow, tied securely to a cottonwood, snorted and pawed the ground. Every once in a while she shuddered, rattling the metal fittings on her saddle and bridle.

Dread and blame vied for dominance in Amanda's churning stomach. She'd been so sure she could handle this ride, so sure it wouldn't jeopardize the safety of her baby. She'd made this trip to Arizona for his safety! And now she'd stranded him in a canyon with a brushfire licking at the canyon mouth. She would have made it out if she could have controlled her mount better, but riding with a cradleboard on her back wasn't the same as riding alone, and Pussywillow had spooked at the sight of the fire.

Amanda's only concern after that was staying on as the gray mare had spun in her tracks and bolted back up the trail. Being thrown on this morning ride hadn't occurred to her. But it should have. She was a stupid woman, an irresponsible mother, she thought miserably. Once she'd realized that Pussywillow wouldn't carry them out, Amanda had decided to wait by the pond. If the fire came up that far, the pond was the safest place to be. She'd wade out in it if necessary. She prayed it wouldn't become necessary.

The bark came again, closer this time, and she stood, her heart beating with hope. Someone was coming! "I'm here!" she called, her voice cracking on the words.

A moment later, a bedraggled Chloe bounded up the path and skidded to a stop in front of her. Tears sprang to Amanda's eyes as she stooped down toward the dog. "Chloe!" A lump lodged in her throat. "Did you . . . did you bring someone with you, girl?" *Chase. Oh, God, let Chase be with you. Please don't have come up this canyon on your own.*

Chloe licked her hand and nuzzled at Bartholomew, who had stopped crying and was staring at the dog. Then he reached both pudgy hands out, and Chloe licked those, too. Bartholomew made a little gurgling noise and waved his arms.

Tears streamed from Amanda's eyes and landed on Chloe's matted coat. "You've brought someone, haven't you," she whispered, refusing to believe otherwise. "I hope so, because we're in bad straits here. I'm very glad to see you, but I'd be even happier to see Chase. Is he with you?"

Chloe whined and wagged her tail.

"Let's go watch for him." Amanda straightened, took a calming breath and walked toward the trail. "Chase!" she called. A hot wind blew up through the canyon and seemed to carry her shout behind her.

"Amanda!" came a reply from below her, down the trail. "Stay there, babe!"

Half crying, half laughing, she hugged Bartholomew to her. "I will!" she called in a choked voice. "Your daddy's coming," she murmured to the baby as she rocked him back and forth. "Your daddy's coming to save us!" She stood on tiptoe, straining to see the winding trail obscured by rocky outcroppings and scrub oak. At last she made him out, moving along the trail, the most wonderful man in the world. "I see you!" she called, waving. Her words echoed against the canyon walls.

"Are you okay?" came the echoing response.

"Yes!"

"Is Bart okay?"

She didn't miss the order in which he'd asked. "Yes! Is the fire bad?"

"We'll make it," he called after a moment.

We'll make it. The echo bounded back and forth, surrounding her, suffusing her with hope and energy. He'd said the same thing when he'd carried her through waisthigh snowdrifts to the truck of his cab. Fate had sent her this warm and caring man to love and protect her from harm, and all she'd tried to do was drive him away. Yet here he was again, determined to bring her to safety.

Warm emotions coursed through her, emotions begging to be released as she watched him climb steadily toward her. Soon he was close enough to glimpse his unshaven face beneath the battered old brown hat. His clothes looked as if he'd slept in them. She'd never seen anyone so handsome in her life.

"I love you," she called, her voice echoing down the canyon toward him.

His head snapped up in surprise. "You what?"

"I love you!" she shouted, making the canyon walls ring.

"Well, I love you, too, you headstrong woman!" He sounded a little angry, a little tense, but he'd said it. He'd said it!

She laughed.

After a moment, his laughter joined hers, rippling through the trees, bouncing off the granite walls. He was still laughing when he dismounted beside her and pulled her into his arms. "Of all the stupid times for you to say that."

"I know." She looked up into his shining eyes.

"You realize we'll have to get married."

"If we get out of this canyon alive, that is."

"Amanda, just shut up and agree to marry me. Let me worry about getting us out of here."

"I'll marry you, but what about—"

He kissed her swiftly. "That's all the time we have for that. We have to douse us all in water and get going."

"Yes, but we haven't settled—"

"We will. Come on. You're going in the pond with me, and so is little Bart. And so is Chloe. Get everything wet."

"Even your hat? You love this hat."

He gave her a crooked smile. "I guess that gives you an idea of how much I love you, now, doesn't it?" he asked softly. "Get in the water."

Amanda followed his directions and they all started down the trail dripping wet, with Chase carrying Bartholomew on his back and leading the skittish Pussywillow.

"We'll leave her if we have to," he said over his shoulder. "We'll try to have you ride her out, but if she won't go, even with Chloe's help, I'm taking you on behind me and sending her back up the canyon."

"Chase, I don't want to leave—"

"You will, if I have to strap you on behind me like a gunnysack. Is that understood?"

She should have been outraged that he'd order her around like that. She wasn't. With every word out of his mouth since he'd appeared on the trail, he'd emphasized that she was the most important person in the world to him. She'd never been that before, with anyone except the little baby riding on Chase's back. It felt wonderful. She still had no idea how they'd work out the details of living together. Giving up her career wasn't an option. *We'll make it,* he'd said. She had to believe they would.

Pussywillow began to tremble as the smoke reached them. Chloe stayed where the gray mare could see her, and Pussywillow kept putting one foot in front of the other. Amanda wrapped herself in the wet blanket as Chase had instructed. As she pulled it over her mouth and nose, Chase adjusted his blanket around Bartholomew.

"There's not much space, but we're going through," he shouted back to her over the roar and snap of the fire.

Pussywillow whinnied and tried to rear. Chase pulled down hard on her reins. "Come on, Pussywillow! Carry that woman through this fire! Chloe's here. Follow Chloe!"

As if in response, Chloe barked, taking Pussywillow's attention away from the flames. As Amanda leaned forward and stroked the gray mare's neck and murmured encouragement, the horse put one shaking leg forward, then another.

Coughing and gagging, they inched along. It's like walking through hell, Amanda thought as she pulled the wet wool blanket over her nose and mouth. Her eyes streaming from the smoke, she kept her gaze fastened on Chase's blanket-shrouded form. *Whither thou goest.* He had never led her astray.

At last the smoke began to clear. When they were several yards from the edge of the blaze, Chase swung the blanket from his shoulders and pulled on Pussywillow's reins to bring Amanda alongside him. "Check on Bart," he said.

Amanda took off her own blanket so she could lean over and peer under the hood of the cradleboard. Bartholomew stared back at her, his eyes solemn, looking for all the world like a green-eyed Indian baby. "You okay, sweetheart?" she murmured, touching his cheek and giving him an encouraging smile.

Bartholomew smiled back.

"He's fine." Tears poured from her eyes. "No thanks to me, he's fine."

Chase turned in the saddle. "Don't you dare blame yourself. You're the best mother I've ever seen."

"I nearly got him killed."

"No, the fire nearly did that, not you."

"But if you hadn't come to save us...."

He smiled. "The thing is, I did. Now let's get out of here before Pussywillow acts up again." He started off, leading the mare behind him.

The thing is, I need you. Bartholomew and I need you, Amanda thought as they rode south and put more distance between them and the fire.

Finally, Chase led them to the top of a rise and pulled Amanda alongside him again. He gazed at her without speaking for a moment. Then he cleared his throat. "Did you . . . mean what you said back there in the canyon?"

Sudden fear struck at her. Maybe it had only been the drama of the moment that had made him say he loved her, that had made him propose and cast away his role as a drifter. "Did you?"

The corner of his mouth twitched a little at that. "Dammit, woman, I asked you first."

She lifted her chin. All right. Let her be a fool, then. "Yes, I meant it. I love you. And I can see that you belong here, not in New York posing for ads. I don't know where that leaves me. Leaves us. But I won't ask you to change anything for me. And I know you think marriage is the equivalent of being branded, so I won't hold you to that offer, either. You're a drifter, but I love you, anyway."

"Does that mean you're going to tell your family the truth about me and about Bart?"

She gazed into his eyes and nodded. "I was pretty mixed up, but love has a way of straightening out a person's priorities. I'll tell them as soon as I get back."

"But I don't want you to go back, Amanda."

Her heart beat faster.

"People drift because they don't expect life to give them anything permanent. My expectations have changed." He reached out and touched her cheek, brushing a fleck of soot away. "When the fire started, I had to fight it because the True Love's become the first home I've ever had. And when I figured out you were up in that canyon, I had to find you because . . ." His gaze searched hers. ". . . you're the first woman I've ever loved."

She caught his hand and held it to her cheek. "Oh, Chase."

"Does that sound like a drifter to you?"

Her eyes misted with happy tears. "No." Holding on to the cantle of his saddle, she raised in her stirrups, leaned over and kissed him.

He kissed her back, his fingers combing through her hair and cradling her head. "I love you," he murmured against her mouth. "But I can't ask you to leave the career you love, just to be with me."

She leaned away from him a fraction. "You let me soak your favorite hat."

"That's not the same—"

"There they are! Kissing like damn fools!" The shout came from their far left. They turned to see Leigh bearing down on them, the rest of the hands behind her.

She reined up alongside Amanda. "Honest to Pete, couldn't you have saved that for later? We've been frantic!"

"Sorry, Leigh," Chase said with a grin. "But we had some things to work out."

"Well, work them out somewhere else. There are helicopters on their way, and each one is carrying about a hundred thousand gallons of water to dump on this fire. Their aim is good, but I can't guarantee it's perfect. Unless you want to experience a hundred-thousand-gallon shower from fifty feet above, I suggest you move it!"

Chase handed Pussywillow's reins to Amanda. "Guess we'd better do what the lady says."

"Guess so."

Leigh led them all a half mile away before turning back toward the fire. "We can watch from here. It should be pretty spectacular. Here they come."

Amanda was transfixed by the sight of one of the helicopters carrying a giant yellow bucket suspended from a long cable. When the helicopter was positioned over the fire, the bucket opened from the bottom and water cascaded over the fire. The blaze hissed and steamed, exactly as if it were a giant campfire. A second helicopter came in and repeated the process on a different section.

"They'll go back and reload, and do it again. With that and the trenches we dug, I think we'll be okay," Leigh said. "The air tankers are standing by in case we need to drop a fire retardant, but we may not need it." She turned to Chase. "So what did you two have to work out that was so important?"

"How we can maintain a marriage when Amanda's working in New York and I'm out here."

Leigh rolled her eyes. "Is that all? Ry and I have that figured out."

"Oh, have you?" Chase shoved his hat to the back of his head. "And when did you do that?"

"I wandered out to the patio the night we all had food poisoning. Ry said you'd gone to the cottage, so we started brainstorming. We figured you two had your minds on less-practical matters."

To Leigh's left Duane gave a snort.

"Go on," Amanda said.

"Ry needed something to do the morning of the wedding. He was driving us all crazy from five on. We didn't want to let him be the one to pick up Belinda and Dexter at the hospital for fear he'd run the van into a tree, so I finally told him to call Amanda's ad agency in New York. He hired them to beef up the True Love's image—something it really needs after all these so-called accidents."

Amanda's jaw dropped. "He's hired Artemis?"

"With the provision that you'll do all the work, and we recommended you be on site. I realize it's not a complete answer to your problem, but it's a start."

"I'm astounded. I don't know what to say."

"You can thank Ry when you see him. He's the one with the mind for these things. I never thought I'd say that a New York mentality would be good for something, but apparently it is."

"You can thank him now," Duane said. "Here he comes, with Freddy right behind him. He musta driven that mountain like he had a burr under his saddle to get here this fast."

Ry charged up the hillside and wheeled Red Devil to look out over the charred desert. "Is it under control?"

"I think it will be soon," Leigh said. "Sorry about the shortened honeymoon."

"No problem." Ry stared at the smoke, which grew lighter in color as the fire began to go out. "Duane, why don't you and the hands ride around to the north and make sure everything's okay in that direction."

"Shore, boss." Duane motioned to the other hands and they trotted away just as Freddy rode up.

"Where are they going?" she asked.

"I sent them off so we could talk in private," Ry said. "Anybody have any ideas how this started?"

No one said anything.

Ry glanced at Chase and Leigh. "Do you think it was set?"

"Could be," Leigh said. "I didn't see any lightning over this way last night."

Ry absently rubbed Red Devil's neck. "And nobody's come across Whitlock this morning?"

Leigh shook her head. "He partied pretty late, too, but you'd think somebody over at his place would have seen the fire and come running."

"Eb wouldn't do this," Freddy said, earning a skeptical look from her husband. "I can't imagine anyone deliberately setting a fire. Even if you could devalue the True Love, it isn't worth the risk."

"It is if you're desperate," Ry said. "I'm beginning to think there's more at stake here than the land."

Leigh sighed. "My instincts tell me you're on to something, much as I hate to admit we have a problem. Look, we've fooled around long enough. How about getting your buddy Joe Gilardini out here to conduct a quiet little investigation? This sort of thing has to stop or we'll lose the True Love."

"That can't happen," Amanda said with a conviction that surprised her.

"Is that so?" Chase's dimple flashed as he glanced at her. Then he turned to Freddy. "Looks like you've won more support for your cause, Mrs. McGuinnes."

Ry coughed. "You all realize that if Joe wants to sell the ranch, we have to sell it." He glanced apologetically at his wife. "I gave my word."

"All the more reason to get him out here," Freddy said. "We'll give him a horse to ride and a mystery to solve. What more could he want to keep him happy?"

"Oh, I can think of something," Chase said with a wink at Amanda.

As if on cue everyone turned toward Leigh.

She held up both hands. "Oh, no, you don't. A New York City Cop? Not in a million years!"

* * * * *

Don't miss the fireworks when Leigh first encounters Joe Gilardini, a cynical cop, who steals her heart in THE LAWMAN, available in November wherever Harlequin books are sold.

HARLEQUIN®

COMING NEXT MONTH

#561 THE LADY IN THE MIRROR Judith Arnold
Bachelor Arms Book 10

Welcome to Bachelor Arms, a trendy L.A. apartment building, where you'll encounter some very *interesting* tenants. While searching for his runaway sister, ex-cop Clint McCreary moves into the B.A.—and odd things begin to happen. One, he sees the ghost. Two, he meets heartbreaker Jessie Gale. Three, he spots a real-life flesh-and-blood woman who resembles the lady in the mirror....

#562 PRIVATE PASSIONS JoAnn Ross
Secret Fantasies Book 11

Do you have a secret fantasy? Desiree Dupree does. By day she's an investigative journalist. At night she lets her imagination heat up and pens erotic love stories. Roman Falconer plays a starring role in her personal fantasies. Except something *scary* is going on in New Orleans and he's the prime suspect....

#563 THE LAWMAN Vicki Lewis Thompson
Urban Cowboys Book 3

A Stetson and spurs don't make a man a cowboy. New York cop Joe Gilardini didn't come out West to ride broncos. He's got an assignment—find who's behind the "accidents" occurring at the True Love ranch. But a tough guy like Joe doesn't stand a chance when the head wrangler, curvy Leigh Singleton, decides to lasso his heart!

#564 ANGEL BABY Leandra Logan

What's a guardian angel to do when her charge isn't fulfilling her destiny? Maggie O'Hara is supposed to marry Timothy Ryan, and despite a lot of celestial maneuvering, Maggie hasn't even noticed him! Well, this is one angel who's prepared to do what's necessary, including coming to earth as an *angel baby*....

AVAILABLE NOW:

#557 PASSION AND SCANDAL
Candace Schuler
Bachelor Arms Book 9

#558 KISS OF THE BEAST
Mallory Rush
Secret Fantasies Book 10

#559 THE DRIFTER
Vicki Lewis Thompson
Urban Cowboys Book 2

#560 MAKE-BELIEVE HONEYMOON
Kristine Rolofson